# DARK FIRMAMENT

## THIRD MOON RISING BOOK 2

E ZRA  E  M ANES

DARK FIRMAMENT

This is a work of fiction. All the characters and events portrayed in this novel are either fictitious or are used fictitiously.

Cover image by Catherine A. Zocco

Cover background image "Center of the Milky Way Galaxy IV" by NASA/JPL-Caltech/ESA/CXC/STScI

ISBN-13: 9781514238141
ISBN-10: 1514238144
Library of Congress Control Number: 2015909491
CreateSpace Independent Publishing Platform
North Charleston, South Carolina

# CONTENTS

# ACKNOWLEDGMENTS

**M**y heartfelt thanks go to my wife, Jan, whose understanding, encouragement, and patience made writing this novel possible while we juggled numerous other important family events and relationships. And once again, I thank family and friends for their encouragement and constructive criticism.

I read a wide variety of current scientific news sources, including *Scientific American, Science News,* and *Astronomy Magazine,* which gives rise to all kinds of imaginative, fictional extensions to current advanced ideas and technologies. The fictional extensions presented herein are solely the author's responsibility.

I am also motivated to let my imagination fly free by the numerous science fiction novels I have read over the years. I seldom start a new story without thinking about a quote attributed to the great author and engineer, Sir Arthur C. Clarke, who said, "Sufficiently advanced technology is indistinguishable from magic." I have endeavored to sprinkle some "magic" throughout this work of fiction.

# DARK FIRMAMENT

*Imagination, creativity, and necessity
drive sentient species
to achieve the impossible.*

# PROLOGUE

Ecina was slender and fast, and escaped Joqi's rushes several times, much to his aggravation. He scrambled around large boulders scattered here and there, chasing his friend in a game of tag. They were playing behind an old iron reinforced wood retaining wall next to some salt pits, which were on the large farm his parents managed.

He was nine years old and Ecina was a year younger; he was stronger, she was faster. He finally cornered her for the tag, and then turned and ran. She chased him in turn through the jumbled boulders.

She was persistent, and to show her up and escape, Joqi started climbing the four meter high retaining wall. It was slow going and she caught him by an ankle before he was a meter off the ground. She held on and pulled him down. They fell together and lay on the ground laughing and pushing at each other. They were oblivious to the constant sound of large machines working steadily on the other side of the retaining wall.

Ecina jumped up and ran. Still laughing, he chased her around a large boulder. A loud clang brought them to a halt; an iron strap on the retaining wall had broken as a machine pushed salt high against the wall. The wall started toppling down on them.

Joqi turned to run to safety but Ecina froze in place. He turned back and grabbed her arm, pulling her away from the wall. They were not going to make it! He pushed her hard away from the wall as he tripped on some loose gravel.

She stumbled but managed to stay on her feet. She ran screaming as he fell next to a large boulder. The wall came crashing down and slammed onto the boulders, breaking apart in several places. The machine operator was slow to notice the wall giving away and continued pushing salt against and up over the broken wall.

Joqi was protected somewhat beside the large boulder, which had a piece of the wall blocking most of the salt from covering him. He was trapped in a small air pocket, buried alive by a thick layer of coarse salt. The total darkness and rank smell of unprocessed salt in the small enclosure assaulted his senses. Powdery salt dust filled the air, making it hard to breathe. His knees were gashed from falling on gravel and the salt burned like fire in the cuts.

His whimpers turned to sobs, and then to screams as his young mind grappled with being trapped in the dark, confined space. Fear grew in leaps and bounds like a demon rising to consume him. He totally lost his sense of being as terror gripped him with burning tentacles. He curled into a ball, whimpering and sobbing as his body convulsed and emptied his bladder.

A calming thought pushed hard at his tightening ball of chaotic emotions. Stronger and stronger the persistent thought pushed, bringing a glimmer of reason into his jumbled young mind.

*Joqi, I am here. Focus on me!*

*Gran...Granpeda?*

*Yes, it is me. Focus on me!*

*Granpeda, help me!*

Two hours later the rubble was removed sufficiently for his father to pull him to safety. Joqi was found sitting calmly beside a large boulder with legs crossed in a meditative position.

This was the first time he exchanged thoughts directly with his grandpapa. He learned years later that his grandpapa had a neural implant that enabled him to communicate telepathically. Joqi did not; his capability came with the rather unique way his brain structure evolved during development in his mother's womb and through early childhood.

# PART 1

# CHAPTER 1

The plea came like a faint morning breeze and Joqi almost missed it.

He paused, pulling back from deep immersion in the design diagram hovering above his workstation.

There, it came again, soft as a shadow cast upon the ground.

*Come, Joqi.*

Joqi turned off the 3-D visualization of the irrigation system he was designing for the cooperative farm his parents managed. He closed his eyes to shut out other visual distractions, and focused his thoughts, reaching out to enfold the wispy, elusive thread.

*Granpeda, are you alright?*

*Come soon, my Joqi.*

With a flick of his forefinger he stored the irrigation system design changes, and then turned off the workstation.

He had communicated with his grandpapa Sepeda at this great distance only once before, and it was under dire circumstances.

"Dad," he called out to get the attention of his father, who was busy at a nearby workstation. "Grandpapa's time is near. We must hurry back to Zilerip."

His father nodded his understanding. He didn't question his son; he had known for many years about the unique telepathic link shared by Joaquin and his grandfather, Prophet Carlos Sepeda.

His father shut off his workstation and opened an intercom link to the farm collective's launch facility. He directed the launch manager to ready their jump-shuttle for departure to the capital city as soon as possible.

Joqi hurried to the community bunkroom to collect his personal belongings. He was glad to find the large room unoccupied. An overpowering sense of dread, of deep loss, surged to the forefront of his thoughts as he stuffed personal items into a travel bag. He stopped and sat on his assigned bed, tears welling up.

*Joqi, you must never grieve for me. I will always be near.*

*Oh, Granpeda...*

*Get a grip on your emotions and hurry home! I sense a looming threat to our civilization. You must act quickly.*

*Me? Why me?* There was no response. He projected thoughts outward and sensed nothing.

He rose and quickly finished collecting his personal things, and then headed for the launch pad. In spite of his depressed state of mind, Joaquin smiled at the memory of his grandfather giving him the nickname Joqi. He was short and wiry as an adolescent, and was always climbing onto things. Back then he loved to ride domesticated farm animals, and the saszu in particular, which led to his grandpapa Sepeda nicknaming him Joqi. A saszu was similar to a horse, and his grandpapa said Joqi reminded him of the jockeys he had seen riding race horses in old Earth video clips. When spoken in English, Joqi's name rhymed with jockey. His grandpapa still called him Joqi, as close family members did, even though he was now tall and muscular, and a respected mechanobiologist and physicist.

The jump-shuttle looked like a mix between an aircraft and a rocket sitting on the launch pad. The shuttle launched and landed vertically on its rocket engines. Joqi rode an elevator to the top of the portable launch structure housing the shuttle, and quickly climbed into the passenger compartment.

His father was already strapped into one of the shuttle's four seats and was talking to his wife via a video satellite link. She was in Zilerip visiting family. Joqi's mother was visibly upset.

"But Rici, your father has shown no change in his condition over the past several months," she said. "I visited him this morning and could see no change."

Horacio Sepeda, nicknamed Rici, turned his hands palm upward. "Kali, we have what we have, sweetheart. We must trust our son's judgment regarding his grandpapa."

"Hi Mom," Joqi said as he slid into the seat beside his father.

"Hi dear," she said. "Tell me what is going on."

"Grandpapa summoned us and indicated it is critically important that we hurry to his side." He paused. "I sensed that he does not have much time left."

She frowned and remained quiet for a few moments. Joqi saw his father entering launch data via the control panel in the arm of his seat.

"I will let everyone know," Joqi's mother finally said, with a catch in her voice. "Love you guys. Hurry back."

The display deactivated before they could respond.

Joqi strapped himself securely in his seat, and his father commanded the autopilot to launch for Zilerip, the capital city of the planet Zilia.

The shuttle's engines growled to life, like angry, wild beasts ready to jump into action. And, like its name implied, the shuttle literally jumped off the launch pad and roared into the dark blue sky under autopilot control.

Joqi grimaced as the 4g acceleration pressed him deep into the padded seat. In a jump-shuttle, you launched and landed while sitting with your back parallel to the ground. This was only his second ride in this type shuttle. He didn't enjoy it any better now than he had the first time.

The high-g acceleration continued until the shuttle was in suborbital flight, where the engines quieted to a low hum. The large collective farm his father managed was about a fourth of the way around Zilia from Zilerip. It would take them about two hours and a half to reach the capital city in the jump-shuttle.

He looked at his father, who had turned to look out a small porthole illuminated by the midday sun. He sensed that his father was already grieving.

Joqi reached over and lightly gripped his father's shoulder. He in turn reached up and patted Joqi's hand. They shared a strong bond, a loving bond, which they often expressed openly. They worked in very diverse professions; one a farmer, the other a scientist, both honored professions on Zilia.

Science was considered an art on Zilia, and artists pursuing advanced studies were held in high esteem. Joqi enjoyed his artistic profession, but was happiest when visiting and working on the collective farm his parents managed. The wide-open landscape around the huge farm appealed to him.

His father turned to face him, grief showing in tear-filled eyes. "We have known the past few months that Father faced this transition soon. I hoped he would make it to the next primary two-moon eclipse."

*That was too much to hope for,* Joqi thought, but couldn't bring himself to say it. The primary eclipse would occur in another five and a half months.

"When talking to Father recently," his father added, "I sensed we were on the cusp of another major revelation."

Joqi remained quiet, although his father was clearly expecting a response. Should he share what grandpapa had conveyed about a threat to their civilization? No, no need to upset his father any more than he already was. After all, he didn't really know anything about the threat his grandpapa alluded to.

"Dad, Grandpapa expressed concern about what we face going forward. He didn't provide details. He urged me to hurry home."

His father frowned at Joqi switching to English instead of speaking Zilanese. But he shrugged, nodded, and turned back to face the porthole. Joqi preferred English; it was more efficient than the melodic Zilan language. English was the language he and his grandpapa used in conversing when they were alone or with Joqi's younger sister, Alandi.

*I should have said "urged us to hurry home"*, Joqi thought. Regardless, he knew his father, the youngest of Prophet Carlos Sepeda's nineteen children, wouldn't take offense. He had never said nor did anything that even remotely showed jealousy or chagrin regarding Joqi's close relationship with his grandpapa Sepeda. On the contrary, he always supported and encouraged that special relationship.

Joqi could see his father's face reflected in the porthole, which now had a backdrop of dark sky above the horizon. It could easily be mistaken for his own reflection, showing an angular jaw, slightly heightened cheekbones, thick arching eyebrows, and a strong, long nose above a thin mustache. His eyes were large, with long eyelashes, and the reflection showed his eyes and hair as black, although they were both dark brown. Slight cheek dimples showed on occasions when his father smiled. If he and his father were the same age, they could be mistaken for twins; that is, if Joqi were to grow a mustache. But at twenty-six years old, he still preferred a clean shaven face.

His father's lips moving silently and Joqi knew he was praying. His father and mother were openly devout in practicing their religious beliefs, as were most Zilans, even government officials. The common religion among those in society was tightly coupled with government doctrine.

Joqi believed in a higher power in the universe, but not to the basic driving level that his parents did. He remained respectfully silent as his father continued to pray.

He smiled for the second time since the summons, again at a childhood memory. At a very early age, he started calling his Grandpapa Sepeda by the nickname Granpeda. Joqi remembered his mother trying her best to get him to call the revered prophet by grandpapa, but he intervened, saying it was special to him that Joqi called him that unique nickname. No one else did. As Joqi grew older, he greeted his grandfather as everyone else in the family did when only family was around, as Grandpapa Sepeda. But when Joqi and his grandpapa communicated privately, he still used the more personal nickname Granpeda.

They had been in flight for almost two hours when Joqi's mother contacted them again by video link from Zilerip. Her face looked strained and her eyes were red, probably from crying.

"Joqi is right," she said. "Your father's vital signs are weakening fast."

"We will land soon," Rici said. "Sweetheart, I believe my father will survive until we get there. Otherwise, he would have summoned Joqi earlier."

Joqi believed that also and was glad his dad thought the same thing.

"I want to believe that," Kali said. "Regardless, I have arranged for flitter transportation directly from the jump-shuttle pad to your father's home."

She hesitated, grasping for words, then her motherly concerns burst forth. "Joqi, why..., why is Grandpapa focusing on you? Why did he summon you directly? Are you in danger? Why will he not answer my questions?"

"Mother, Grandpapa indicated we all face a looming threat going forward from today."

His father looked at him sharply. Uh oh, what he said was a little more serious than what he told his father earlier.

"The only way I know to get answers," continued Joqi, "is to get to Grandpapa as soon as possible. I have tried communicating with him, but to no avail."

It was clear his words had not relieved his mother's concerns. Nor could he think of anything else he could say to ease her state of mind.

For the remainder of the flight, Joqi shared the quiet solitude with his father while remembering the good times experienced with his extended family and his grandpapa in particular.

• • •

Joqi's mother greeted them at the front entryway to Prophet Sepeda's home.

"Oh, Rici," she said, as she rushed into her husband's arms. They hugged close, and then she turned her attention to Joqi.

"We must hurry," she said, giving Joqi a quick hug. "Grandpapa keeps asking for you both."

As they turned to go, Ecina Cenenteh rushed into the entryway and into Joqi's arms.

"I love you," she whispered. "Please hurry. Grandpapa is slipping fast"

He had known Ecina as a good friend for many years, but had only started dating her a year earlier. She was a descendent of Caron Cenenteh, a respected Zilan physician that had worked closely with Prophet Sepeda's team upon their arrival on Zilia. Joqi's strong friendship with Ecina blossomed into love very quickly. He had proposed marriage during the last two-moon eclipse, two months earlier. Their marriage was scheduled to occur in five and a half months at the peak of the next Holy Seven-Year Two-Moon Eclipse.

He held Ecina close for a moment, and then followed his parents into the large greeting room of the home. Close family members, senior clergy, and government representatives were gathered in small groups talking in hushed tones. The room quieted as they entered. Many of his first cousins were present, plus all his siblings; his younger sister and three older brothers.

Joqi's parents nodded to those close by as they hurried across the room, with him following close behind.

*Oh, Joqi.*

Startled, Joqi stopped. That intruding thought came from someone other than his grandpapa. Looking around, he was drawn to his sister. She had such an anguished look on her face!

*It will be okay, Alandi.*

Now it was his sister who was startled. She was unaware that she had communicated with him. Until this moment, only he, his grandpapa, and the artificial intelligence entity Eve were known to communicate this way. The grief of the moment had freed Alandi's mind to reach out to him.

11

Joqi smiled at her, then projected, *Keep this secret until we can talk.*

She nodded, surprise still showing on her face.

He turned and followed his parents into the private quarters in the back half of the home.

# CHAPTER 2

*Granpeda!*

Joqi projected the involuntary thought outward when he saw his grandfather's gaunt, ashen face. Was he still breathing? He lay limp on top of the bed covers with only a light, dark-blue nightshirt on his frail body. His arms lay motionless along his sides and his head and shoulders were propped up on pillows. His high priest ceremonial tunic lay across his feet, the rumpled, dark-blue material trimmed in gold lace looking no less regal.

A slight smile formed on Prophet Sepeda's face and his eyes fluttered open, causing murmuring to ripple among those holding vigil in the room.

The large bedroom was in semidarkness with only dimmed lighting over the bed. Joqi's eyes adjusted quickly to the dimness as he and his parents approached the bed. It looked like all eighteen of the prophet's other children, all sons, were crowded into the room. The prophet having all sons by his two wives was considered a minor miracle. The sons' birthdays spanned a period of thirty-five years.

The High Priest of Zilerip, Olinza Harsn, stood on the opposite side of the bed. She was outfitted in formal high priest attire; dark blue clothing and a blue cape trimmed with gold colored lace. She looked trim and proper, as she had every other time Joqi had seen her.

"Bless you, my son, my Rici," whispered Prophet Sepeda as Rici gave him a gentle hug. "Be strong as you give up Joqi to his mission."

Joqi's mother sucked in her breath sharply and reached over to grip his arm.

*My mission?* Confused thoughts raced through Joqi's mind as whispering spread throughout the room and then quickly subsided.

"My Joqi," his grandpapa whispered. He beckoned with a trembling hand.

Joqi patted his mother's hand and she released his arm. He moved quickly to tenderly grasp the prophet's feeble hand. He dropped to his knees beside the bed and kissed his grandpapa's hand. Leaning slightly forward, he looked into dark brown eyes that exuded wisdom and solemn confidence. Joqi was so choked with emotion that he couldn't speak.

"All here must bear witness and attest to what I say," said Prophet Sepeda, in a surprisingly loud voice. He looked around at his children and the High Priest. "A terrible danger hovers close by, one which imperils all humankind, not just our Zilan civilization."

The room remained surprisingly quiet, although Joqi could see the tension and concern in the faces of those standing close about.

The prophet held out his other hand. Joqi's mother leaned over and handed him a folded and sealed single sheet of paper. She stepped back, tears streaming down her cheeks.

Prophet Sepeda handed the paper to Joqi. "You and Dawn must be at this location at the peak of the next two-moon eclipse. This is the critical first step in countering the imminent dark danger."

The prophet again addressed those assembled. "Joqi has within him the knowledge and wisdom to do what is necessary. You must give him your full support."

The 139 years old prophet's eyes closed and his hands went limp. Several of those present began weeping.

Joqi felt numbness forming inside, as if to suppress his grief. Why select him? Was there no other information? What was the nature of the danger? Who was Dawn? He closed his eyes and bowed his head to hide his confusion and the tears welling up.

*Granpeda, what is this danger, what must I do?*

*You will know, my Joqi. I will watch over you.*

*Please stay, Granpeda. I need your guidance and wisdom.*

*Trust your instinct, your intuition. Joqi, always remember your leadership role in advancing our society.*

Joqi's thoughts reached out in anguish, trying to maintain the link with his grandpapa's thoughts, which were dissipating in death like wispy fog rising to greet the morning sun. It was no use; his queries were quickly lost in a void of darkness.

Gasps and murmurs of awe from those nearby caused Joqi to raise his head and open his eyes. A shimmering, moon-like sphere of bright light hovered above his grand-papa's head.

*Granpeda!* He shivered and goose bumps danced up his arms and across his back.

His father knelt beside him and placed a hand on his right shoulder. His mother did likewise on his left.

Joqi felt a mental nudge to hold out his hands, palms upward, and he complied. The radiant sphere began moving, crossing slowly from above Prophet Sepeda's head to hover above Joqi's hands, shining brightly like a full moon. The sphere suddenly brightened more, causing him to instinctively close his eyes.

A panoramic view spread out before him. He was high above pearly white clouds, looking at a bright sun starting to set at the horizon. The sun was much brighter than their local sun Arzét. He stood on firm ground, on a rocky, barren mountain top. He shivered in the cold, acrid air, which smelled of sulfur. He needed oxygen and drew in deep breaths of the thin air, even though it burned his throat. He knew of no place like this on Zilia.

*Grandpeda, is this where I must go?*

Receiving no answer, Joqi opened his eyes as the panoramic vision dissipated. The bright sphere lay nestled in his open palms. It dimmed to full moon brightness, and in a blink it was gone.

A respectful silence pervaded the room for a full minute. High Priest Harsn looked at Joqi questioningly, and then began reciting the Prayer of Deliverance. All in the room joined in, including Joqi. The respectful prayer eased the transition to the spirit world, and was considered most effective when delivered as soon as possible after someone started the journey.

After the prayer, the High Priest, and then each of Prophet Sepeda's sons, approached the bed and touched the prophet on the arm, giving a touch of respect and taking a touch of peace, as was the Zilan way.

As the others filed out of the room, Joqi remained kneeling and holding his grandpapa's limp hand. Memories of the prophet's two wives came to mind. Gloria Ceyam Sepeda and Ceripe Largena Sepeda had preceded him in death many years before. Surely they were waiting to greet his grandpapa in the spirit world. Joqi had known his kind grandmothers in his childhood days, but didn't remember much about them. Ceripe Sepeda was his maternal grandmother.

He sensed the presence of another.

*Eve?*

*Yes, Joaquin. I have stayed close to Prophet Sepeda this past year, at his request. His transition leaves a great void in our world. I am now at your service.*

Joqi looked more closely at the room. In the dim lighting, he could just make out a small camera pod in the corner at the ceiling of the wall behind the bed headboard. The pod provided Eve video access to the room; however, she could communicate directly with Joqi.

He and his grandpapa were the only ones that could link directly with Eve. She was the artificial intelligence that had achieved sentience during the journey to Zilia with his grandfather over a century earlier. And now perhaps another could communicate with Eve as well—Alandi.

Joqi rose, still holding his grandpapa's limp right hand. He positioned the prophet's arms and hands so the fingers intertwined on the center of his chest, the position he had seen so many times when his grandpapa meditated or prayed.

*Did you record the small moon moving from Grandpapa to me,* Joqi asked.

*Yes,* Eve replied. *I will provide a copy for High Priest Harsn. Who is Dawn?*

*Dawn and I are one and the same. I will explain this and many other things soon,* Eve projected. *I leave you now.*

Joqi touched his grandpapa's arm reverently, and then sat in a meditative position on the floor. He lost the battle to control his emotions and his shoulders heaved with each sob.

• • •

Joqi's father, mother, and High Priest Harsn greeted him in the hallway outside his grandpapa's bedroom. His mother and father hugged him together, and then stood close beside him, each holding one of his hands. His mother squeezed his left hand so hard it hurt; she was taking loss of the prophet hard, plus now having to deal with Joqi's selection to lead what must be a dangerous mission.

High Priest Harsn stepped forward to touch Joqi lightly on both arms. "Our hearts are heavy this day, but we are thankful we had Prophet Sepeda to guide us through the past century."

Joqi could only nod his agreement. He didn't know the high priest very well, but his father and mother held her in high esteem.

"Did Prophet Sepeda convey additional information about the imminent danger," the priestess asked, dropping her arms to her sides. She was aware of Joqi's telepathic ability. "You appeared to experience something when the sphere hovered in your palms."

"A…dream-like vision came to me, of a place like none I can imagine existing here on Zilia." He explained in detail what he had experienced.

"Before the sphere appeared," Joqi continued. "I asked Grandpapa what the dark danger was, but he was circumspect in his answer. He said I would know and to trust my instincts."

Joqi hesitated, and then added, "He would have told me if he knew more." He bowed his head and said, "Why me?"

"Joqi, we must trust your grandfather. His visions have always borne truth and guided us well." The High Priest smiled and touched him on both arms again. "You were chosen for good reasons, even though all are not apparent now."

Joqi nodded numbly. Were there no answers? Was he to blindly march ahead?

"Have you opened the sealed paper," his father asked,

"No, Father." He searched his pockets for the paper. "I must have left it with Grandpapa."

They followed him back into the bedroom. High Priest Harsn smiled and nodded her approval of how he had placed the prophet's hands. She picked up the sealed paper from the side of the bed and handed it to Joqi.

"I request you share what is written inside with our Council of Priests and our Supreme Leader, when you are ready."

Joqi nodded and without hesitation broke the seal on the folded paper. The hand-drawn markings confused him for a moment, and then he understood. His grandpapa had drawn seven reference points in space. Three of the points clearly represented the alignment of their planet Zilia with its two moons at the next Primary Two-Moon Eclipse, which would occur in five and a half months. This set the time reference for location of the other points.

Each of the other four points had a solid line emanating into space, with a specific angle annotated next to each point. The lines converged at a point in the outer reaches of their solar system. The line emanating from Zilia's outer moon to the intersection point was a dashed line. The intersection point must be where his grandpapa wanted him at when the next two-moon eclipse peak occurred.

He looked at his grandpapa laying as if in a deep sleep. *I understand, Granpeda. I will be there as you wish, if at all possible.* He did not expect, nor did he get any reply.

He focused attention back on his parents and High Priest Harsn. He held the drawing up for all to see.

"The drawing depicts a coordinate system with seven points of reference identifying a specific location in space and time. The reference points are distant stars plus the planet Zilia aligned with its two moons."

His father leaned closer. "The stars are not identified. The one closest to Zilia must be our sun, but what about the others?"

"I believe the reference points refer to stars in our neighborhood of the Milky Way galaxy," Joqi replied. "We must run simulations to find stars that fit the time and angles referenced by the intersecting lines. This process will quickly locate and verify the reference points."

There were more lines crossing at the intersection point than were necessary to locate the point in space, which could mean one or more of the lines had additional significance. He decided to hold off bringing up this point; hopefully the significance would become apparent once the referenced stars were identified.

"The moons are perfectly aligned with Zilia, as they will be in our next Primary Two-Moon Eclipse," the High Priest said. "As you know, this is also our next Holy Seven-Year Two-Moon Eclipse."

The High Priest frowned and looked closer at the drawing. "Prophet Sepeda must have drawn this some time back. The annotations are in his handwriting and are crisp and smooth. He was unable to write this way the past several months in his weakened condition."

Joqi nodded slowly. He had an uneasy feeling that the timing of his grandpapa's death had great significance to the mission that lay before him. They had five and a half months to get to the intersection point.

Apparently the High Priest was having similar thoughts. "The religious symbolism is very important to solidify support for your mission," she said. "May I take this drawing to show to our Council of Priests and the Supreme Leader?"

What was this, the High Priest asking his permission? And she had mentioned the supreme leader twice, which made Joqi wonder why Ciasan Tojmera was not present, as other key officials were.

"Certainly, I would feel better if you safeguarded the original copy. But I need to place a working copy on file where it will be accessible to those helping get me to the location specified."

He held the paper up so it was clearly visible to the camera pod.

*Eve, please copy and save this drawing.*

*It is done,* Eve conveyed. *I will start the simulations to find the reference stars and the intersection point.*

Eve paused, and then added, *Joaquin, you and your mission are now my top priorities.*

Joqi handed the drawing to High Priest Harsn, who looked him squarely in the eyes until he became uncomfortable. She was looking for some response from him, but he had nothing else to say.

"Do you recall viewing the recordings of the Third Moon Rising miracle when you attended religious services as a youth," the High Priest asked.

Yes he did, and the memory raised goose bumps again. He nodded slowly.

"Seeing the bright sphere hover above Prophet Sepeda and then your hands," she added, "reminded me of that most holy event that occurred over a century ago."

"Eve will provide a recording of the sphere moving from Grandpapa to me," Joqi said.

"I hoped she would," the priest said. "Thank you."

The High Priest touched him lightly on the arm again before leaving the room. To have the "touch of respect and touch of peace" administered by the high priest of their religious order was unnerving, to say the least—as was thinking about the Holy Third Moon Rising event.

He turned to comfort his mother, who was crying again. "Why you," she whispered through soft sobs as he held her close.

# CHAPTER 3

"**I**s there no other way?"

Joqi's question seemed to linger in the air like a foul mist; some in the room fidgeted, others found somewhere else to look, avoiding his eyes. The one at the front center of the assembled group did neither. He was tall, with dark black hair, and sported an impressive mustache that curled at the ends. Lenjay Genai, launch project manager, looked at Joqi stoically for a full minute before giving a response.

"Not if you are to get there at the appointed time," Lenjay finally said. "I would recommend launching today if the ship was ready. But a few modifications are necessary if you are to survive the journey."

*I agree with Lenjay,* Eve conveyed privately. *Prophet Sepeda pushed hard the past two years to get the* Horizon Quest *outfitted with the latest technology. Now I understand why.*

Joqi shook his head, slumping back in his chair. The plan was crazy, but it was the only feasible approach to get him and Dawn to the exact point his grandpapa's drawing depicted at the specified time. It required launching the Space Agency's research vessel, the *Horizon Quest,* no later than four weeks hence. And to top it off, it would require full acceleration all the way to the intersection point for another four months.

The first stage acceleration would be provided by detachable, outboard pulsed fusion engines to conserve onboard fuel. They would jettison the outboard engines after accelerating for one month, and then the onboard pulsed fusion engines would take over. The problem was that full acceleration resulted in a sustained g-force that far exceeded what a human could withstand!

In addition, the *Horizon Quest* would arrive at the intersection point at a very high velocity. The pulsed-fusion engines could slow the spaceship after reaching the target point, but it would take considerable time. So, how were they to engage whatever the threat was at the intersection point while traveling at a significant relativistic velocity?

It had taken two weeks after Prophet Sepeda died to come up with this approach. It was the only possible way with current technology to get to the intersection point at the specified time, now just five months away.

Joqi was sorry he was unable to participate more in the mission planning activities, but there was no way he would miss his grandpapa's funeral and ceremonial spreading of the prophet's ashes over farm fields. In addition, the mission planning process was clearly a very challenging engineering problem with time constraints, requiring an experienced team from the outset.

Once the intersection point was defined, ground based and orbiting satellite sensors were used to scrutinize the point and space near it. They looked for any objects or anomalies that might be there—nothing was found. They continued to monitor the intersection point and expanded the search into neighboring space.

Joqi focused attention back on the mission launch team, which had remained respectfully silent as his ruminations ran their course. The team expected him to make the decision to proceed. After all, he was elevated to the position of Mission Commander by the last words of Prophet Sepeda. And he would be the one running the risk on the mission. Right now the mission was to get to the intersection point on time. After that, well, who knew?

"Okay," he said, sitting up straight. "I assume you have started preparations knowing this is the only way."

Lenjay let a smile flicker across his normally solemn face. He had taken a liking to the prophet's grandson. "Yes, we are pushing ahead as fast as we can, at Eve's insistence."

"I thought that was what you and Prophet Sepeda would want," Eve said.

Joqi nodded. "You need to bring me up to speed on what must be done, including what I need to focus on to support the mission."

Lenjay told all the others to get back to work. He and Eve would go over the plan details with Joaquin.

"When will you create Dawn," Joqi asked Eve. Dawn would be a copy of Eve transferred into the *Horizon Quest's* advanced computing and neural networking systems.

"It has in effect already occurred," Eve responded. "I exist in both places, and think, perform, learn, and respond as one. That will change upon launch of the *Horizon Quest*. The duplicate segment of me onboard will function and respond independently as Dawn."

"Will Dawn be as capable as you," asked Lenjay, and then he grimaced, recognizing the naivety of his question.

"Of course," Eve replied evenly. "Upon our separation, Dawn will have all the memories and extensive data records that I have. Dawn will continue interacting and evolving as a new entity. You can change Dawn's gender identity if you wish."

"That is not necessary," Joqi said. Lenjay nodded his agreement.

"I understand your engineers want to strip much of the research equipment from the *Horizon Quest*," Joqi said, addressing Lenjay. "Does this include the high power lasers?"

Lenjay frowned, and said, "Yes, removal of the laser systems and several minor systems will significantly reduce the mass that must be accelerated initially by the external pulsed fusion engines. This will increase the safety margin for arriving at the intersection point on time."

Joqi was not in favor of removing the lasers at all. He recalled from Zilan history that such lasers were used to intercept an alien probe many decades earlier, causing it to crash into the sun. The lasers were the only weapons aboard the ship; two forward, two aft, and two at mid-ship.

Without them the ship would be defenseless. They would just have to accept less safety margin.

Joqi gave a measured response. "The *Horizon Quest* was built with Prophet Sepeda's guidance. Everything onboard is there for a purpose yet unknown. I want everything left as is unless you consider a change absolutely necessary for us to get to the intersection point on time."

"As you wish, Joqi," Lenjay said quietly. "I will clear any changes through you before proceeding."

"There is a compromise worth considering," Eve said. "The ship has very capable, reconfigurable robots that can fabricate or manufacture about anything."

"That is right," Lenjay said. "Some of the robots onboard were used to help build the ship."

Eve paused at this interruption, and then continued. "We could remove the two mid-ship laser systems. The forward and aft lasers can cover over 90 percent of space around the ship. Full coverage can be achieved by repositioning the ship slightly. The two mid-ship laser systems could be fabricated later if needed."

"If there was time to do so," Joqi said. He mulled over what Eve said. Her approach was reasonable. The lasers were there to destroy any asteroids in danger of hitting the ship. Ship defense for other threats was a secondary priority, albeit an important one considering the mission.

"Okay, remove the mid-ship laser systems," he said. "But check with me on any other changes."

"Now, how do you make a spaceship pilot out of a scientist in one month," Joqi asked, thick brown eyebrows deeply furrowed.

This caused Lenjay to laugh outright for the first time in Joqi's presence. Joqi smiled, easing the tension.

"Sorry," Lenjay said. "It struck me as funny that the guy that invented the smart plasma would ask that question. We are modifying the *Horizon Quest* to incorporate a plasma full-immersion pod for spacecraft control. It will also minimize the effects of high-g acceleration."

Joqi stood abruptly and started walking back and forth. The answer was the smart plasma, of course. It would provide the interface between him and all the *Horizon Quest's* sensors and controls. He had proven quite capable in directly testing the liquid plasma as a control interface in a laboratory setting. But this would be total immersion in a command pod filled with the smart plasma!

The plasma was comprised of a clear organic liquid that hosted nanobots, stem cells, T-cells, dissolved minerals, and other materials required for sustenance and maintenance of a person's health. By orchestrating electrical, mechanical, and chemical interactions at the cellular level, the smart plasma nanobots could stimulate tissue and organ growth of any type in Joqi's body. In addition, the plasma could stimulate the thousands of bacteria hosted by his body to produce a wide variety of individual cells that would produce antibiotic and other agents to maintain and promote body health. The plasma was self-sustaining and self-perpetuating, drawing from stored resources. Theoretically, a person immersed in smart plasma would not age, at the price of living in a virtual reality environment.

"Dawn is fully capable of controlling the *Horizon Quest*," Eve said. "And she will be in constant contact with you, except when you want private time."

"In spite of this," Lenjay added, "it is imperative that you spend several hours a day immersed in the plasma over the next month to adapt to that interface medium. You will learn how to access and operate the key control systems and ship sensors before launch. After launch you will have another four months before reaching the intersection point to learn how to control the systems with finesse."

Joqi stopped next to a table at the front of the room. Beads of sweat collected on his furrowed brow. Goosebumps began doing a dance on his back. He leaned on the table and placed both hands on it, palms down. The thought of being confined in the pod immersed in the plasma elevated his claustrophobic fears.

*Breathe, Joaquin,* Eve conveyed privately. *Focus your thoughts on what we must do. Prophet Sepeda explained this fear you have, one he fought all his life. Like him, you can control the fear.*

He felt a hand on his shoulder.

"Are you okay," Lenjay asked.

Joqi took a deep breath before answering. "Yes. Please give me a few minutes. Then we can proceed."

"I will check on our team's activities, then we can resume," Lenjay said softly. He touched Joqi lightly on his arm and then departed.

Joqi sat down in the chair he had occupied earlier. He closed his eyes and rested his head in his hands. He could tell that Eve had also withdrawn. The childhood memory of being trapped under a construction wall came rushing back. He felt the raw fear experienced when first buried under the broken wall and coarse salt. Then he relaxed and smiled at the soothing memory of his grandpapa coaching him to meditate to control his claustrophobic fear while buried alive.

He sensed the presence of Eve again.

*May I let Lenjay know you are ready to continue,* Eve asked.

*Yes, I am ready. But I still have no desire to immerse myself in the smart plasma.*

• • •

Joqi looked across the dinner table at his mother's solemn face. She had decided to stay at grandpapa Sepeda's home to help organize the prophet's large cache of notes, essays, and other writings, before turning them over to the Council of Priests. His father had returned home to resolve some issues at the collective farm they managed.

"I am so worried about you, Joqi," she said, frowning. "What is this danger you seek? When will you return?"

"I don't know what we seek. I trust Grandpapa and will do as he asked."

"I know, Joqi. I know." She was having trouble fighting back tears. "But why must you go, why not one of his nineteen children or an experienced pilot?"

"I don't know," he replied, then noticed his answer had caused her frown to deepen. Uh oh, he had answered in English instead of the Zilan language. Why, he didn't know. She thought English was an archaic, common language, considering all its contractions and lack of rhythm. He had learned English from archived training courses. They were brought to Zilia long ago by his grandpapa's team from the distant Messier Colony on the planet Hope. He realized he often thought in English; to him it was a more efficient language.

"I have something very personal and important to ask you, Mother."

She cleared her throat and dabbed at her eyes with a napkin, and looked at him quizzically.

"I want to marry Ecina before leaving on this mission."

"No, Joqi…" She sat back, and then smiled. "Yes, I can see why you would want that. You will be far out in space at the peak of the next two-moon eclipse."

Then she leaned forward, frowning again. "You don't think you'll return from this mission, do you?"

He laughed with gusto. She had replied in English. His laughter caused her to pause, and then her frown turned to a transient smile, which turned to laughter. He reached across the table and clasped her hands in his.

When their laughter subsided, he said, "I love Ecina dearly and want to hold her close before I depart. I'll cherish that throughout the mission."

"Then go to her, son. Go soon!"

· · ·

Joqi was deep in thought while riding in the back of the transit railcar to a stop near Ecina's apartment. He hardly noticed others coming and going as the railcar stopped periodically along the way. He was having difficulty assimilating all that had occurred in the past week since the first meeting with Lenjay and Eve. He was very uncomfortable transitioning from his role as a scientist to that of mission commander, in spite of everyone's support and encouragement.

He had never considered himself as being overly special. Sure, he had provided the theory that led to development of the smart plasma. And he had advanced the Zilan understanding of the physics of the observable universe and some inferred unobservable dimensions. But those achievements paled in his mind in comparison to the research and advances that enabled development of spaceships like the *Horizon Quest*.

He shook his head to clear somewhat chaotic thoughts as the railcar approached his stop. He had spent very little time alone with Ecina since his grandpapa died. She would be his only wife, as it should be. His father was of the last generation in which multiple wife marriages were sanctioned on Zilia. But his father chose to have only one wife, and Joqi was glad.

Joqi's grandpapa and the Council of Priests had stopped sanctioning multiple wife marriages three decades earlier. Multiple wife marriages were encouraged for several centuries before that time to counter the decline in population due to male infertility problems. Prophet Sepeda's team discovered the cause of the infertility soon after arriving at Zilia. An isotope in crushed mining aggregate residue used for centuries in the initial filtering phase of water management facilities was absorbed, causing male infertility.

Joqi focused outward as the railcar stopped. The only other people in the car were a young couple sitting next to the exit with their two children, a boy about ten years old and a girl about eight. Joqi smiled and nodded to the couple as he rose and prepared to exit. To his surprise, the young boy stood up and touched him lightly on the arm. The little girl did likewise, followed by the mother and father. He nodded to them again and exited the car, his unease heightened by the encounter. He had seen this happen many times to his grandpapa, but why was it happening to him? In spite of his unease, he appreciated their touch of respect and of peace.

Nightfall was setting in as he approached Ecina's apartment, which was one half of a duplex house. She shared the apartment with her parents when they were in Zilerip. They had returned to a large cooperative farm after Prophet Sepeda's funeral.

Ecina had a window open even though the night was getting chilly. He paused at the sound of her singing a pleasant ballad. It heightened his anticipation for having a wonderful evening with her. Walking to the front door, he could see her busily preparing something in the kitchen. She was wearing a light-green tunic which complemented her auburn hair. She came quickly when the entryway announced his arrival.

She opened the door and met him with a big smile and a close embrace. Their long, deep kiss set him afire in ways that were pleasant and disturbing. He wanted her now! But that was not the Zilan way.

"I've missed you so much," she said, looking up at him with her gray-green eyes. He could see the love in them and a bit of mischief as well.

"I've missed you also," he said. "The thought of being without you for several months has disturbed me more than I can say."

She looked at him curiously, and then smiled. "Then we need to make the most of the time we have."

She stepped aside to let him enter, but he wasn't ready to let the moment pass. He pulled her close again and she brushed up against him with her ample breasts, and then pushed him away playfully.

"Go to the living room. I'll bring in some tea and cakes." She chuckled as she headed to the kitchen.

She had never been this forward in all their dating. They had touched intimately on occasion, but never with the sensual teasing she showed tonight. They had always practiced restraint while looking forward to the day they would be married.

He sat on the living room couch trying to ignore the physical byproduct of Ecina's passionate greeting. He smiled at the realization their conversation was conducted in the English language. She knew he favored that language, and was using it more and more when they were away from others.

Ecina came in a few minutes later carrying a tray with tea and small cakes on it. She had removed her light tunic, revealing a low cut, lacy white blouse that flared out over a silky knee-length skirt. She was barefooted, as she often was when inside. Her swollen nipples pushed against the thin blouse material—she wasn't wearing a bra!

She placed the tray on the table in front of the couch and poured him a cup of tea, then one for herself. He was afforded a clear view of her deep cleavage as she leaned over pouring the tea.

She snuggled in beside him on the couch, and they sat sipping tea quietly for a few moments. The tea was very good; she had added just enough brandy for flavoring.

He set his tea back on the tray, and then eased off the couch into a kneeling position before her. She looked at him questioningly as he took her tea cup and set it next to his. He pushed the table carefully back away from the couch.

"Ecina, I want to marry you," he said huskily, leaning against her knees.

She smiled and placed her hands on his shoulders. "Of course you do, silly. We're engaged."

"No, I want to marry you now, before I leave on this mission!"

He saw confusion in her face, then it cleared and she smiled.

"I want that as well. I was prepared tonight to…, well, to get to know you a lot better."

He smiled and nodded. Her actions had revealed as much.

"How soon are you talking about," she asked.

"In a matter of days, if our parents agree," he replied, "We are set to launch the ship in three weeks."

She spread her legs and pulled him close. Their tender kiss turned passionate, and she lay over on the couch, pulling him over beside her. The taste of her mouth and feel of her probing tongue melted his resolve to practice restraint until they were married.

He stroked her smooth legs, pushing her skirt up to her hips. She responded by snuggling closer as he tenderly touched her inner thighs. They were warm to the touch and silky smooth. He moved his hand higher—no panties!

Ecina gasped as he touched her most sensitive area and pushed him away. "Joqi, I cannot…"

Joqi rolled off the couch and sat on the floor breathing heavily. "I'm sorry, sweetheart," he said, in a voice ragged with passion. "I got carried away."

"I did as well," she said, sitting upright and smoothing her dress. "I wanted to go all the way tonight." She leaned over and cupped his face with her hands. "We need to consummate our marriage as soon as possible!"

He nodded. "My mother already supports this and I'm sure father will as well."

"I'll get my parents approval tomorrow," she said.

He kissed her gently, then rose and departed, one of the hardest things he had ever done.

# CHAPTER 4

Joqi watched fascinated as the smart biomechanical plasma climbed slowly up his arm. The pinkish, slightly iridescent plasma covered all exposed skin as it spread higher. It felt like a million small insects were climbing and covering his arm. In essence that was true, although most were nanobots. He straightened up abruptly, shaking his arm to dislodge the climbers. They dropped back into the tank without hesitation. His arm felt wet and dirty even though neither was the case.

"What is wrong," Eve asked via a video terminal. "You have touched and handled the smart plasma many times in the laboratory."

At his request, only Eve was monitoring this test activity in the Research Laboratory of the Institute of Advanced Studies. It wasn't touching the liquid plasma that was the problem. He had yet to convince himself he could lay down fully immersed in a plasma filled command pod. But that was required for him to survive the trip to the intersection point.

"I'm not sure I can do this," Joqi replied hesitantly.

It was called smart plasma because it had self-organizing skills enabling it to adapt and perform a wide range of functions. The smart plasma's host medium, a synthetic pink tinged fluid, was almost translucent. It functioned much like the colorless fluid part of blood, in which cells and minute particles necessary to maintain the health of organisms were suspended. In the smart plasma, the suspended particles were Joqi's genetically modified t-cells and stem cells, plus nano-size robots, or nanobots. The plasma contained other basic ingredients necessary to interface with and maintain the health of immersed entities—in this case, him. The cells and nanobots operated in cooperative swarms, or colonies, to perform the many tasks necessary to provide life support and maintain ship systems interfaces.

"You must, Joaquin," Eve said firmly. She always called him Joaquin.

*Remember your first swim in a spring fed river.*

*Granpeda?* There was no answer to his query. His imagination must be working overtime.

He smiled at the memory of standing on the bank of the Avili, a spring fed river running through the co-op farm his father and mother managed. At ten years old, he had already learned how to swim in the warm water in farm tanks. This was different. He could sense the coldness of the clear spring water pooled downstream from some rapids. He started to dip a foot in the water, but his grandpapa stopped him.

"Joqi," he said "if you test the water you will not want to go in."

So he had jumped in, and came up flailing around and gasping for air. The sudden shock of immersion in the cold water took his breath away. By the time he swam back to shore he had adjusted and was ready to go back in.

"Okay, Eve, I know what I must do."

He stepped over the tank's side and lay down quickly, immersing his nude body in the plasma. His heart raced so fast it felt like it might jump out of his chest. He gasped for air and there was none as the plasma closed over his mouth and nose. It took all his will power to stay submerged and stop trying to breathe while the plasma adjusted to his needs.

He finally had to breathe, and did so, pulling in air from a bubble the plasma formed over his mouth and nose. He drew in several deep breaths, and then forced his thoughts into a meditative mood, slowly relaxing as the mood deepened.

The plasma encased him as would a protective fluid around an embryo. But the plasma did much more, monitoring his vitals, repairing skin damaged by sunlight and scratches, and seeking out all body sensory interfaces: touch, smell, hearing, taste, sight and psychic. The plasma interfaced directly with his brain using low power electromagnetic coupling. This latter function would enable him to interface with and control all the spaceship functions.

Joqi didn't want to think about another aspect of the smart plasma. It would gradually enter all orifices of his body if he stayed immerse long enough, providing nutrients and oxygen as needed, disposing of waste material, and healing any maladies he might contract.

This invasive feature, coupled with the sensory and direct mental interfaces, would transition him to a virtual environment, a realistic virtual existence as long as he was submerged in the plasma. He shuddered at the thought of interfacing with the plasma to this extent and tried to block any interaction with the plasma that would suggest going to full invasive immersion.

He lay meditating as the plasma fully acclimated to his presence. He felt light as air, as if floating in a huge, dark chamber that had boundaries he couldn't sense. He thought about Ecina and her image appeared as realistic as it was the night before, including her teasing, seductive smile. He started reliving the encounter with her, as clear and as real as it had been the night before. His body ached for follow through!

He forced his thoughts away from Ecina, seeking out the external interfaces to the plasma test tank. He could see the interior of the test facility in which the plasma tank was placed. He saw Lenjay Genai enter the facility and walk to the edge of the tank.

"How is he doing, Eve," Lenjay asked.

"I will let him answer that," Eve replied.

Joqi smiled as he realized the plasma had connected him with a video interface.

"I am fine, Lenjay," he thought/said.

Lenjay stepped back abruptly from the tank, and then smiled in embarrassment at his reaction. "Okay, I knew you could do that."

Joqi experimented with other interfaces as Lenjay and Eve monitored his actions. He accessed and controlled all automated systems in the test facility. Then he found interfaces to links outside the facility. He watched through distant optical interfaces as materials for the *Horizon Quest* were carried into space by an equatorial space elevator.

He would also ride the elevator up when it came time to board the ship. The space elevator design was brought to Zilia long ago by his grandpapa's team from the planet Hope. Such elevators were used by Earth for over two centuries to provide materials and workers to support orbiting factories and tourist resorts. Joqi was still amazed every time he watched an elevator climb the thick, metamaterial cables. The cables were anchored by strong stanchions in a ground station located along the equator. The space end was tethered to weights positioned just beyond the geosynchronous orbit distance from the surface. Platforms were positioned along the cables at various altitudes in space to support orbiting facilities.

Joqi searched until he found the cameras located on the space elevator unloading station fixed in geosynchronous orbit along the taut elevator cable. Accessing these video cameras, he viewed the huge, orbiting Sayer Research Station that housed the *Horizon Quest*. The research station was named in memory of George and Amanda Sayer, Prophet Sepeda's close friends that accompanied him to Zilia from the planet Hope a century earlier. Joqi remembered his "Uncle" George and "Aunt" Amanda from his early childhood because of the liquorice candy Aunt Amanda was famous for making. Uncle George always had a piece to give to Joqi when he visited.

Joqi could see very little of the research spaceship, for it was docked along the centerline of the revolving, wheel-like research station. The artificial gravity provided by spinning the research station enabled personnel to work and live aboard it for extended periods without suffering physical degradation caused by weightlessness.

He watched as robots ferried material from the unloading station to the research station. He knew that most of the material was to support modifying and outfitting the *Horizon Quest*. Joqi had visited the research station several times, but had never paid much attention to the spaceship nestled in the belly of the station. Back then he viewed the spaceship as just another research module of the large station. He was curious about how the ship was coupled to the station, so he searched until he found a video feed from a robot that was meticulously inspecting the *Horizon Quest*'s exterior surface.

He discovered the ship was held in place by the research station's very sturdy mechanical struts strategically located along and around the ship's hull. He remembered now, the spaceship was capable of relocating the research station in orbit around Zilia and elsewhere. The station could be placed in orbit around the inner moon, or even another planet in the Zilan solar system. The retractable struts had to withstand the force exerted by the maneuvering spaceship.

Joqi did a quick tour of the *Horizon Quest* and accessed its design specs stored in core memory. The research vessel was beyond cutting edge technology; the ship design leapfrogged the spaceship technology brought to Zilia by his grandpapa's team a century earlier. The hull was a long sleek design with an outer layer comprised of metamaterial that could withstand the abrasive impact of minute particles when the ship accelerated to high velocity. The so-called vacuum of space actually contained molecules and very small specs of dust that could wear away the hull as the ship traveled significant distances at high velocity.

The ship had to protect against another threat brought by exposure to outer space—damage to organic material and other sensitive components, like computer systems, by cosmic radiation, high energy particles. Joqi noted this protection was provided aboard the *Horizon Quest* by sustaining electromagnetic spheres, EM bubbles, around sensitive systems and cargo. The EM shields were actually strengthened by impinging ions, mostly protons and atomic nuclei, found in cosmic radiation. The smart plasma command pod was protected by an EM shield, as were the sensitive systems in which Dawn would reside.

The command pod was located on the inner surface of a cylindrical compartment. This compartment could rotate around its centerline, creating an artificial "spin-gravity" on the inner circular surface. This gravity would help maintain Joqi's health and enable him to walk around the cylindrical "floor".

He looked at the inventory of materials being loaded aboard the ship and was surprised to see large quantities of self-assembling components needed to build various reconfigurable robots. But then, with only him aboard, he could envision a multitude of tasks that would require robot support, from ship repairs to mining asteroids to replenishing raw materials required for, among other things, engine fuel and life support systems. As Lenjay told him, the robots could even manufacture more robots with various skills, if needed.

Joqi next accessed the broad-bandwidth links between the orbiting Sayer Research Station and ground research facilities. He focused on what the large telescopes aboard the orbiting station were viewing. Two of the telescopes were focused on the mission target, the intersection point just outside the solar system that was defined by Prophet Sepeda's diagram. To the surprise of the research facility scientists, Joqi took control of one of the telescopes and began searching a broader area looking for anything that might reveal a threat to Zilia.

He was like the proverbial kid in a candy store, turning from one exciting discovery to another. Time seemed to stand still as he continued exploring the wonders he could sample via the smart plasma. He accessed a high resolution imaging satellite that monitored Zilia's surface, and began looking at vast cooperative farms passing under the satellite's field of view.

The satellite images faded away abruptly. He coughed to clear his itchy throat and opened eyelids that wanted to stay stuck closed. He lay on cushioning at the bottom of the test tank. The plasma had retreated!

Joqi sat up and Lenjay handed him a soft white robe.

"I wasn't ready to end the session," Joqi said matter-of-factly.

"I know," replied Lenjay. "That is a major worry we have about using the plasma. The experience can be addictive."

*To say the least,* Joqi thought, and then he said, "I will deal with that aspect as best I can."

• • •

Ecina entered the small meditation room with arms crossed to cover her exposed breasts. She made no effort to cover other private areas. Joqi was afforded a clear view of where his hands had roamed only once before, and his body reacted accordingly, in spite of his efforts to remain calm and relaxed. Ecina's mother was surely watching.

The chaperoned viewing was customary for couples preparing for marriage. Zilan religious and social doctrine required that each partner must view the other's physical attributes and acknowledge acceptance of those attributes before they took the marriage vows.

Ecina smiled nervously and slowly dropped her arms to her sides. Her nipples were either responding to the slight chill in the room, or she was experiencing as much excitement at their pre-marriage viewing as he was.

She looked him in the eyes, and then glanced lower and blushed. Well, she most certainly knew he approved of what he saw!

She turned slowly to afford him a good view of all her attributes. He looked her over from head to toe, and itched to get closer, to touch her again. His private parts ached even more with desire by the time she faced him again.

She smiled, and then her lips silently formed the words, "Your turn."

He turned around slowly, feeling a little light-headed from the rush his pounding heart was causing. This had to end soon or he would lose self-control.

Ecina was beyond blushing—her face was flushed and her chest rose and fell quickly, telling of her heightened arousal.

Joqi forgot for a moment where he was and stepped forward reaching for Ecina. She responded likewise, but both halted their advance when the door to the room opened.

"Oh no, you must wait," Ecina's mother said sternly as she entered carrying two robes. She shook a finger accusingly at Joqi and tossed a robe at him. After wrapping a robe around Ecina, she gave him another stern look and pushed her daughter toward the door. She stopped at the door after Ecina had gone and looked calmly back at Joqi. Then she smiled and exited the room.

Joqi waited a few minutes to let his excitement wane before returning to the opposite room where his chaperone, his oldest brother Rauli, waited. Joqi couldn't help blushing as Rauli smiled a knowing smile. He turned his back to Rauli and pulled on his underwear and trousers. He was having trouble suppressing his desire for Ecina.

# CHAPTER 5

"**S**on, what is it like to fully immerse in the smart plasma?" Startled at the abrupt change in direction of the private conversation with his father and oldest brother Rauli, Joqi leaned back in his chair contemplating how to answer his father. His brother straightened up in his chair at the end of the desk. Why this sudden change from discussing the marriage ceremony?

"I experience an elevated sense of being, of integration with my environment like never before. It is amazing!"

He paused as the implications of this statement pressed to the forefront of his thoughts.

"It makes me want to sense more of my environment, to expand the virtual existence I feel growing around me while in the plasma."

His father frowned. With elbows resting on the desk between them, he began tapping the fingertips of one hand against the fingertips of the other. It was a nervous reflex Joqi had seen many times when his father contemplated problems.

"Father ..." His father held his right palm up to quiet Joqi. His brother Rauli remained respectfully silent.

After a full minute or more, his father said, "Son, are you sure you can handle long-term immersion in the plasma?"

Uh oh, someone had surely told his father about the addictive nature of immersion in the plasma. Probably Alandi, since she was involved in the smart plasma development.

After a measured pause, Joqi answered honestly. "I am not sure. I have experienced full immersion only three times, including this morning. We will know more after a few more sessions."

His father was frowning again and tapping his fingertips together. He stopped tapping and opened a desk drawer. He pulled some papers from the drawer and slid them across the desktop to Joqi.

"Few people know about this research," his father said, "and that is probably for the best right now."

Joqi grimaced as he looked at the title of the research paper—his research paper. "Possible Effects of Human Immersion in Smart Plasma" was never formally published, and for good reasons. A major conclusion of the research paper was that the smart plasma would periodically induce a state of mind much like deep meditation, a proven holistic method of fostering better mental and physical health. The depth of the plasma induced meditation was the concern, with the probability it would stimulate significant physiological changes, especially in the brain.

Joqi had practiced meditation conscientiously since the episode at age nine when the salt pit wall had collapsed on him. Positive effects of practicing meditation, such as improved memory, cognitive skills, and physiological wellbeing, were known for centuries by the Zilans. Research since Prophet Sepeda and his team arrived at Zilia revealed that practicing deep meditation could also rewire some brain neural networks, making them more efficient, and could grow more brain tissue in areas supporting cognitive skills. The smart plasma carried deep meditation to a whole new level, with a probable side effect of immersion addiction.

"I can handle the plasma," Joqi stated emphatically. "My theoretical work enabled creation of the plasma. I am well aware of the possible consequences of full immersion."

What else could he say? Joqi waited patiently for his father to speak.

It was Rauli who spoke instead. It was the first time he had said anything since the conversation turned away from planning the wedding ceremony.

"Joqi, there is something you can try that should help." Rauli reached for the research paper and Joqi handed it across.

Rauli flipped through the first few pages, and then said, "It is quite possible the one thing promoting immersion addiction can also be used to counter that side effect."

Joqi was suddenly all ears. If only there was a way! He wouldn't admit it, but he was already missing being in the smart plasma he had left just a few hours earlier.

Rauli explained that it would do no good to fight the plasma induced deep meditation cycles. But what Joqi could do was control what occurred during the induced meditation. Rauli suggested that in at least half the meditation cycles, Joqi should focus on entering a very personal, very positive virtual existence. He must convince himself that it was his totally private place. He should choose and create a virtual environment that would take him far away from thoughts about smart plasma immersion, especially during long periods of inactivity aboard the *Horizon Quest*. In essence, he would channel his plasma enhanced perceptions about self and his heightened sensitivity to everything external, to create a place in his mind's eye where the plasma was nonexistent. That would build mental stepping stones to freedom from the plasma when he must leave it.

This sounded like convoluted reasoning to Joqi, but it was worth a try. After all, Rauli was a highly respected practicing psychiatrist.

"You can handle it," his father said firmly as Joqi sat digesting what Rauli said. "Still, I have grave concerns about what the plasma immersion will do to you in the long term."

"I do as well, Father. I'll try what Rauli suggested."

"Do you remember undergoing a thorough medical exam when you were ten years old," his father asked. He stopped tapping his fingers and looked Joqi straight in the eyes.

"Yes."

How could he forget; the exam was necessary before starting his first year of crossball play in school. Crossball was a rigorous game requiring manipulating a spherical ball with your feet and body, without using your hands, across a grassy field defended by an opposing team. The game was made more challenging by the ball having an offset, liquid core that caused the ball to react irregularly when hit. The objective was to kick the ball through a one meter loop that was positioned atop a four meters high pole at the end of the field. Scores counted only if you were no closer than twenty meters to the pole. A semicircle of radius twenty meters was marked on the field around the loop pole. The game was more than rigorous; he still carried scars on his legs from wounds inflicted by defenders.

"We never told you about the brain scan your grandpapa Sepeda insisted you undergo back then."

"What...why was it done," Joqi asked.

"I suspect it had something to do with what you face now. Your grandpapa had this uncanny ability to sense things relevant to future events. The scan showed you have many more processing hubs in your brain than are in other people. This probably explains your telepathic capabilities."

Joqi was very familiar with the structure and operation of the human brain from his formal schooling and later research with the smart plasma. In most key areas of the brain, neurons cooperated to form processing hubs that greatly enhanced the brain's effectiveness. Having more processing hubs would surely increase the mind's stochastic processing capability, the ability to quickly find solutions to complex problems given limited random data about the problems.

He didn't know what to make of this new information about his own brain. He had never felt more special than others in his age group; different, yes—more special, no. At times his family elders made him feel special, but that was no big deal. They made all in the younger generation feel special in their own way.

It was surprising the scan was done at all considering the strong Zilan aversion to investigating inside a person's body. But then, Prophet Sepeda had great influence.

"Why are you telling me this now?"

"I want you to know and believe that you have the best chance of anyone on Zilia to meet and overcome the dire threat my father is ... was so concerned about. Challenge yourself mentally and look at problems from different angles. Like your grandpapa said, trust your intuition when you are unsure about what to do."

It was a lot for Joqi to take in. "I am firmly committed to this mission."

"I know you are. But have you given serious thought to what you could do if you focused the full capabilities of your mind?"

No he hadn't, but he certainly would now. He already knew he could "sense" other's thoughts if he concentrated hard enough. He had also demonstrated some psychokinetic ability, moving and deforming small objects by shear mental power. He had never shared knowledge of these capabilities with anyone, although he suspected his grandpapa knew.

He recalled his recent discovery that Alandi could also communicate telepathically. She had sought him out a few times since their grandfather's funeral to practice her emerging capability. His father probably didn't know about her capability or he would have said something. It was best to let Alandi tell him when she was ready.

"Father, I'm sure my full capabilities and Dawn's will be tested in facing the unknown threat."

His father struggled to control his emotions; he had just lost his own father and was now at risk of losing his son.

Joqi wasn't sure just when he had switched to English while talking to his father, and he continued in that language now. "I've been too busy to think much about the personal consequences of the mission. I'm caught up more each day in the rush of activities preparing for our launch date. And I'll spend more and more time immersed in the smart plasma, where I can most effectively support pre-launch activities."

"Just be careful and maintain your personal identity," his father said, his voice strained by emotion. "Let your sense of self anchor you in the real world. Let it pull you back to reality once your mission is completed."

• • •

Joqi felt uneasy ascending the west stairway to the holy top level in the Temple of Zilerip. Normally only the Council of Priests had access to the top level. Considering that Prophet Sepeda had picked Joqi for the mission, High Priest Harsn wanted to personally perform Joqi and Ecina's wedding ceremony.

The High Priest also wanted to highlight the church's approval of the wedding because it was occurring before the next two-moon eclipse phase, the time when weddings were traditionally conducted. But this was not the time to stand on tradition; Prophet Sepeda had died only one month earlier and Joqi's mission would launch in another two weeks.

His oldest brother Rauli greeted him at the closed west door to the Council of Priests chamber. They had to wait until invited inside. Joqi wondered if Ecina was waiting anxiously at the east entryway with her oldest sister.

The door slid open and a priest motioned them inside. As they walked through the door, Joqi saw Ecina and her sister entering through the east door. Ecina looked radiant in a simple white ankle-length dress. High Priest Harsn stood in front of a low alter running along the south wall of the chamber. Joqi and Ecina were escorted to positions facing the High Priest. His and Ecina's parents were standing along the north wall with the supreme leader and a few other high ranking dignitaries. He would rather have more of his and Ecina's family there than the dignitaries. The chamber was devoid of furnishing, and the only decorations were the dark-blue and gold drapes covering the north wall.

Zilan marriage ceremonies were normally simple affairs and the High Priest followed this tradition for Joqi and Ecina. They were asked to link arms, his left arm around her right arm, symbolizing linking them for the rest of their lives. The priest then offered the Bonding Prayer, recounting commitments binding the two together in holy matrimony. They were then asked to hug one another close, as they should the rest of their lives. The priest then touched each lightly on their arms, giving a touch of respect and taking a touch of peace, concluding the ceremony.

Each of the others in attendance approached to touch their arms lightly before filing out of the chamber. The high priest touched their arms lightly again and wished them the best in their joint pursuit of happiness and obedience to Zil, their name for God. She then turned and departed, leaving Joqi and Ecina alone in the holy Council of Priests chamber.

Joqi hugged Ecina close again, whispering in her ear, "I love you."

"Oh, sweetheart, how I've waited for this moment," she whispered back.

They left the chamber with arms linked, heading to the traditional dinner where their families also merged to offer support for their future together.

Joqi and Ecina sat with arms interlocked as they rode the transit railcar to Ecina's apartment after dinner and visiting with their parents and other family members. They planned to stay in Ecina's apartment until after his mission and then move to a house. Several other people were in the railcar. There were knowing smiles here and there when people looked at the newlyweds. But no one intruded on their personal time.

The sun was setting as they left the railcar station and walked to their apartment hand-in-hand. Joqi pulled Ecina close once they were in the apartment entryway and out of sight of anyone outside. She responded passionately to his kiss, pressing hard against him as his hands explored down her backside. There would be no holding back this night.

Ecina pulled back breathless. He wanted more, to breathe her essence in deeply, and he pulled her close again. He wanted to touch her everywhere at once, but settled for feeling her body molded to his as their kiss deepened.

Ecina pulled away, chuckling at his unrestrained groping. "Give me a few minutes, then come to the bedroom."

It was all Joqi could do to restrain himself. He finally gave in and hurried to the bedroom, stopping abruptly at the open door. Ecina stood naked at the foot of the bed, smiling invitingly. He started removing his clothes while drinking in her beauty and sexuality with his eyes.

"I started to put on a shear nightgown," Ecina whispered, "then I thought about your reaction in our nude viewing."

Joqi tossed aside his underwear and looked over his shoulder.

"Is your mother going to stop us this time?"

She laughed and pirouetted in a complete circle. When she completed the turn he stood only a foot away. She was breathing heavily as he pulled her to him and sought her tender lips. The kiss deepened and he moved his hands slowly down her backside.

When the ecstasy of the moment became unbearable, she lay back on the bed and welcomed his passionate advance.

# CHAPTER 6

"**O**ur prelaunch training approach is not working," Lenjay said.

"What do you mean," Joqi asked, even though he knew the answer.

"Limiting the smart plasma to external body interfaces is inhibiting your full access and control of ship sensors and systems."

"I know," Joqi admitted reluctantly.

"You need to go to full invasive immersion and stay there through launch," Eve said, cutting to the bottom line. "It is just six days until launch and you are not ready."

Joqi had come to the same understanding earlier, but procrastinated on making the transition decision. To give up his close relationship with Ecina right after their wedding was a sacrifice he was reluctant to make. And knowing that the smart plasma would enter his body during full, invasive immersion disgusted him.

"Joqi," Lenjay said softly, "the timing of this is terrible, I know, but ..."

Joqi raised his hand, stopping Lenjay from saying anything else.

"We'll go to full invasive immersion tomorrow. I'll say my goodbyes tonight."

• • •

Joqi was more than a little depressed as he made the short walk from the railcar station to the apartment Ecina shared with him. The sky was fighting to hold on to the last light of day, as he was fighting to hold on to every moment of his last day on Zilia. He and Ecina were married just four days earlier and this would be their last night together until after the mission was completed.

His parents and siblings understood why he must proceed with full immersion now, but still, parting was most difficult. He had agreed to visit Alandi in her laboratory the next morning before heading up to the *Horizon Quest*. She wanted to show him an important research project related to sensory perception.

He could see Ecina through the kitchen window, busy with something on the counter. He paused; she was wearing the same outfit as the night they had almost given in to their desires before they were married. She looked beautiful in the light green tunic. He opened the door and entered. She heard him and hurried to greet him.

"I need to talk to you, sweetheart," he said solemnly, cupping her face in his hands.

She pressed close, put a finger on his lips, and shook her head no.

"I've made some tea and cupcakes," she whispered, her voice catching. Seeing the redness around her gray-green eyes, he knew she had been crying. "I'll join you in the living room."

She knew, but how? He walked slowly to the living room, thoughts in turmoil.

He rose from the couch when Ecina came in carrying a tray with tea and cupcakes on it. She handed the tray to him, and he placed it on the table in front of the couch. By the time he straightened up, she had removed the light green tunic. She wore the same lacy white blouse and knee-length loose skirt as before, and her sensual appearance aroused him. She moved quickly to embrace him. In spite of the depressing news he brought her this night, she was focused on making the night memorable for both of them.

"Ecina...,"

She put a finger on his lips again to stop any conversation. The love and desire he saw in her eyes compelled him to kiss her tenderly, to hold and caress her, the love of his life. He soon found out she wore no panties this night either.

Joqi and Ecina cuddled close the next morning, not wanting their intimate time together to end.

"I would like to have a child for each time we made love last night," Ecina whispered.

"That would be a lot of mouths to feed," Joqi said, chuckling.

She laughed and he hugged her close one last time. Ecina pulled away and punched him playfully, and then rolled over to face away from him, fighting back tears. He kissed her on the nape of her neck and got up to shower and dress.

• • •

Joqi found Alandi busy in the biology lab of the Zilan Institute of Advanced Studies. The Institute was located in what was formerly the embassy occupied by their grand-papa Sepeda and his team upon arrival at Zilia as envoys representing Earth. This original diplomatic envoy was still the only humans of Earth origin to visit Zilia. And for good reason; Earth tried to make martyrs of Prophet Sepeda and his team.

Alandi looked up when he entered the lab, and he could tell from her eyes that she had been crying. Two other researchers were working nearby.

Alandi hurried over to greet him with a hug. "I'll miss you, big brother. Thanks for coming to see me."

*I love you sis,* he conveyed. *I'm sorry I have to leave, especially now.*

*I understand,* she responded. *It would be great to cultivate this capability with you.*

*You can communicate with Eve,* Joqi replied. *She will help you hone your skill. And I will converse with you when I can before launch.*

He sensed something or someone else touching his thoughts.

*Alandi?*

*No,* she replied, smiling. *Let me show you something very peculiar.*

The other two researchers were looking at them curiously, since no words were spoken after Alandi's initial greeting.

"Show me what you are working on," Joqi said.

Alandi looked puzzled. She looked at the other two and realized why he was speaking out loud.

"Come, I'll show you." She pulled him by the arm to the glass container she was standing by when he came in. It looked like a fish tank, but without water.

"See that little guy on the rock?"

To Joqi, it looked like an elongated rock itself. It had no visible appendages or body openings that he could see. Its body color was splotchy, a mix of different shades of gray. It was elongated like a stubby snake or long slug.

"Hmmm, no appendages, no visible body openings. I've never seen anything like it."

"Nor have we," Alandi said. "Apparently it eats by absorbing nutrients through the skin and excretes waste the same way, like sweating through the skin. It was found recently in a deep cave near our southern hemisphere mining district."

*But what's really interesting,* she added privately, *is we cannot find any sensory features on or in the little guy. And it has no distinctive internal organs.*

*I sensed the presence of something earlier,* Joqi conveyed. *Was it this creature?*

*I believe so, but I haven't shared this with anyone else.* Alandi then continued, "We three have been looking closely at this one and several of its kind. So far we are baffled as to what it is or what it can do."

"It seems to sense its environment in some uncommon way," said one of the two researchers. He smiled, and then added, "We have jokingly nicknamed it the ESP slug."

Joqi smiled back. The "extrasensory perception slug", a name probably more appropriate than the researcher realized.

Alandi nodded toward another door and motioned for him to follow her into an office. She closed the door for privacy.

"I wanted to see you before you are ensconced in the command pod," she said. "But I also wanted you to see the slug. It's about as alien a creature as you'll find here."

She struggled for words and for composure. Before she could continue, Joqi gathered her in his arms for a long hug.

*I will be okay, Sis. I understand your concern and the message you want to convey.*

*Joqi, keep your mind open and alert for all things peculiar. Something as innocuous as a slug may open the door to unbelievable surprises.*

His little sister was surprisingly mature.

*I'll keep an open mind, Sis.*

He hugged her close again, and then left. He couldn't delay any longer; Lenjay and Eve were waiting to seal him in the plasma filled command pod. Then in one week the *Horizon Quest* would launch, heading toward the intersection point.

• • •

"Until we meet again in person, my friend, stay safe," Lenjay said as Joqi stepped into the command pod aboard the *Horizon Quest.*

"I will never be far away," Joqi replied as he watched the smart plasma flow quickly up his naked body. He fully expected to stay in close contact with those on Zilia via the Hycoms communication links.

He reached over and touched Lenjay on the arm. "Thanks for giving me as much time as possible with my family before starting fulltime immersion. I will learn what I must know by launch time."

"I know you will," Lenjay said as Joqi lay back and submerged in the plasma filled pod.

Joqi relaxed as the pod hatch sealed shut, and of all things, he thought about the "ESP" slug Alandi had shown him earlier in the day. In a way he was like the slug when he was immersed in the plasma. The plasma formed a homogenous shell around him in the command pod, with no visible interfaces with the external environment. He communicated with the shell; it communicated with everything external to the pod.

He opened his mind to the plasma and encouraged it to establish deep, direct contact with all his sensory elements, something he had heretofore not done. Joqi thought about his grandpapa, and for the first time fully accepted that his role in the mission was essential for its success. This acceptance kept him relaxed as the plasma entered every bodily opening while establishing contact with every nerve ending in his skin, internally and externally.

Joqi focused his mind to sense the vibrant virtual environment established by his full integration with the smart plasma. His experience with immersion in the plasma before this had only scratched the surface of the capabilities and vision brought to bear in the expanded virtual environment.

*Now you are beginning to understand what is possible with full immersion,* Eve projected. *But I caution you, this brings with it higher risk of immersion addiction, as was addressed with you by Rauli and your father.*

*I feel more capable, more powerful, than ever in my life,* Joqi replied. *And yes, I understand that addiction is a very real concern.*

But Joqi's focus was already turning to exploring all aspects of the *Horizon Quest's* systems, and Eve sensed this. It was time to give birth to another.

*Joqi, this is Dawn. I am at your service.*

• • •

Joqi's hunger for knowledge grew dramatically as the hours passed. The more he learned about the ship and its extensive suite of systems, the more he wanted to learn. And he quickly discovered how to tune the subtleties of the virtual environment he now lived in to improve the fidelity of the experience. The smart plasma was remarkable, but it had never existed in any environment other than a containment tank until integrated into the command pod.

The initial virtual environment the plasma established for Joqi was impressive, considering it was developed based on observations, not on interactions with him. Once he learned how to provide feedback to the plasma, the virtual environment quickly evolved to be as real as anything experienced in his daily life on Zilia. Adding to the experience was the broad spectrum view he now possessed when accessing all the *Horizon Quest's* sensors.

*Talk about a realistic virtual reality, nothing can beat this!* His thought was a casual one, but someone picked up on it quickly.

*Total immersion does indeed make a difference,* she observed.

It was Eve but not Eve. Somehow he could tell the difference.

*Yes it does, Dawn. And I'm getting over the initial discomfort of having the plasma interface more intimately with me.*

He realized he had communicated using English. It didn't make any difference to Eve or Dawn what language he used. But his thoughts and communications were more focused and efficient when they were in English.

*For the duration of our mission,* he conveyed, *I want communications between us to be in English.*

*As you wish,* she replied. *Must I use the slang, contractions, and other idioms of the English language?*

Joqi smiled and replied. *Not at all, Dawn.* It appeared that Eve's offspring was developing a personality uniquely hers.

At the start of the second day of full immersion, Joqi slowed his racing mind enough to contact Ecina as she started her day. Her smile and bubbly conversation with him showed how much she appreciated his taking the time to interact with her. He felt and shared his love for her as best he could under the circumstances. But he soon sensed a nagging pull to focus again on learning all he could about accessing and operating shipboard systems. In parting, he promised to contact her early each day and again at night until the ship launched. He kept his promise.

Joqi far exceeded Lenjay and Eve's expectations in quickly learning how to operate ship systems and pilot the vessel. It helped greatly to have a partner aboard that was every bit as capable as Eve—Dawn, the clone of Eve. Dawn came with full knowledge of ship systems and how to maneuver the *Horizon Quest*. With Joqi's intuitive grasp of how to best assimilate sensor data, they made an excellent team.

To Joqi, the launch of the *Horizon Quest* was anticlimactic after the frenzied activities required to get the ship and him and Dawn ready for launch. He accessed cameras on the space elevator platform and looked closely at the group of family members and Zilan leaders assembled. He could see a full range of emotions portrayed on the faces, from confidence and hope to worry and anxiety. His father stood proudly in the front with one arm hugging Joqi's mother and the other hugging Ecina, who was losing the battle to control her tears.

All his goodbyes were said; all the ship preparations were done. He withdrew from observing those on the platform as Dawn eased the ship out from its central position in the orbiting Sayer Research Station. She deftly turned the vessel to engage the trajectory outward toward the intersection point. Joqi activated the external pulsed fusion engines when the ship was at a safe distance from the research station.

*Godspeed, my Joqi, have a safe journey.*

# CHAPTER 7

The pitch black ball hovered motionlessly near the floor in the mist shrouded enclosure. The chill in the air did nothing to improve Joqi's mood. With a sense of foreboding, he reached out toward the black ball, but stopped when it started to flatten. The ball's surface now looked shiny, perhaps from the mist wetting its surface.

What was this? A slight bulge appeared at the top of the object and then moved down across the surface nearest him. The ball flattened even more and expanded outward horizontally at the middle. It elongating out toward him as it settled to the floor. Other small bulges appeared on top of the flattened object, moving haphazardly around the surface.

No, not just bulges. Something, or some things, moved around just under the elongated ball's skin. It didn't look like a ball any longer; if it had legs it would look like a big black bug, thick and rounded at the end nearest him and thin and narrow at the other end.

Something punctured the black skin from the inside and a nauseating smell engulfed Joqi. Other puncture holes appeared in the skin. The rotten smell was so strong he couldn't breathe. And then small, black, insect-like creatures crawled out of the puncture holes.

Joqi backed up quickly and banged against a cold metal wall. His movement or the noise he made attracted the attention of the small black insects. They swarmed as one toward him. He looked around quickly but there was no where he could go to escape. He covered his face with his hands to protect his eyes and exposed tender flesh.

The pain was excruciating as the creatures bit into his legs, arms, and hands...

Joqi sat up, shaking from the fear that lingered from the bad daydream while in deep meditation. The smart plasma reacted to remove the sweat that would have drenched him had he been in a normal bed. The virtual environment came back in focus swiftly.

"Was it the same dream," Dawn asked.

"Yes," he replied. "But this time the creatures swarmed over me and started biting my flesh."

He had shrugged off previous similar episodes while meditating as being side effects of adjusting to immersion in the smart plasma filled command pod. But he couldn't shrug off this last dream; it had been too real and had gone past the point of his just feeling threatened. The little black creatures had started eating him!

Thankfully Dawn remained quiet, giving him time to think things through. He looked outward using the sensors of the *Horizon Quest*. The spaceship was still accelerating quickly away from Arzét, Zilia's star, which they had used to slingshot the ship toward the rendezvous point, the intersection point depicted on Prophet Sepeda's map. They would continue accelerating all the way to that point for another month.

A memory link popped into sight near the ship virtual controls and monitoring indicators. He smiled. This was Dawn's way of interacting when unsure if she should interrupt his thought processes.

He accessed the information identified by the link and would have jumped out of his seat had he been in one. The image in the information was a larger manifestation of the small creatures that attacked him in his daydream!

The rest of the information was sketchy, but identified the creature as a Clac, a crustacean-like alien creature, whose home world was located out in the Sagittarius region of space. The Clac planet orbited around a bright star located about 118 light-years from Zilia. Discovery of the Clacs was the reason Earth sent the first emigrants into other solar systems.

He had an uneasy thought. "How did you know to highlight this particular data set?"

"There was a striking likeness between the Clac and the small creatures in your dream," Dawn replied.

"You can monitor my dreams through the smart plasma interface!"

Dawn made no response to his sudden revelation.

"I should have known," he said, trying to suppress his rising anger. His daydreams about intimate time spent with Ecina were an open book to Dawn. As was his weekly communications with Ecina and family.

He stood up in his virtual environment, looking for something to lash out at physically, and just as quickly, he knew this was the wrong way. He assumed a sitting, meditative position on a padded floor, with legs crossed and arms folded across his chest. A part of him still knew he was immersed in smart plasma. But for all practical purposes, the virtual environment became whatever he needed, including simulating Ecina when he needed to hold her.

Dawn finally spoke. "I stop monitoring your interaction with the plasma induced virtual environment whenever it becomes clear you want private time. However, the plasma alerts me when you experience trauma, even in a dream. My focus is on maintaining your health."

This was a reasonable approach to monitoring his activities. And he had never seen even an inkling of interest on Dawn or Eve's part to intrude on private thoughts or actions.

"I understand," he said, his tension quickly draining away.

"I will change my monitoring activities however you wish," Dawn said.

"No change is necessary."

Joqi switched to a direct link with Dawn to bypass the verbal communication impediment. Dawn acknowledged the link immediately.

He focused on the Clac information, which he didn't know Dawn had obtained. He discovered she had acquired and stored as much information as possible regarding activities, technology, and conditions on Earth and its colonies before the *Horizon Quest* launched from Zilia. She had hacked into data banks on Earth and its two major colonies in other solar systems to obtain the latest information, including what was known about the Clacs. Earth had deciphered the Clacs' verbal language, which Dawn could code into a translator aboard the *Horizon Quest*, if needed.

Dawn's research, including the hacking, was done via Hycoms links. The *Horizon Quest* had an advanced hyperspace-communications capability, Hycoms, as they called it, enabling almost instantaneous communication even at interstellar distances. This communications technology was brought to Zilia by Prophet Sepeda and his team, and enhanced by Zilan scientists.

Prophet Sepeda's team also brought an extensive library of information about stars in the Milky Way galaxy, including great detail for the stars in the Sagittarius Constellation. These stars had an abundance of planets orbiting them as compared to other regions of the galaxy reasonably close to human occupied worlds. Sagittarius had another very interesting factor—when viewing the constellation from Zilia, you were looking toward the center of the Milky Way galaxy. Zilan astronomers were thrilled to get this library information, and consequently adopted the Earth nomenclature for the stars.

Joqi used the *Horizon Quest's* long range, full spectrum scanners, to scrutinize space around the intersection point closely. There was no indication that any Clac vessel was anywhere in the neighborhood of their destination. In fact, there was nothing visible at or close around that point.

Joqi had mixed emotions about whether to notify those back on Zilia of his dreams and the concern the Clacs might pose an imminent threat. Dawn reminded him of the great importance Prophet Sepeda's dreams had played in ensuring the survival of the diplomatic team sent by Earth to Zilia two generations earlier. He reluctantly agreed to share his dreams and concerns, but with only select members of the Zilan religious order and the supreme leader's staff, plus Eve and his father.

• • •

Five individuals were seated around the large conference table, including the Supreme Leader, Ciasan Tojmera, at the far end, with High Priest Harsn on his right. Joqi's father sat to the right of the high priest. The leader's chief-of-staff, Marih Basira, sat on his left, and then Lenjay Genai, now the Mission Coordinator. And of course, Eve was present via video link.

Joqi projected his 3-D simulacrum, a lifelike representation of himself, over a Hycoms link. Dawn monitored proceedings over the same broadband communications link. He assimilated his simulacrum standing at the near side of the table, opposite from the supreme leader.

"Thank you for meeting with such short notice," Joqi said.

"Your mission is our mission," Ciasan Tojmera said. "And the mission is our highest priority."

"I have had recurring dreams recently that could be significant regarding the threat mentioned by my grandfather, Prophet Sepeda." His abrupt statement commanded their attention. They all waited in attentive silence for him to continue.

"Dawn, please show them."

A 3-D visualization of his latest dream materialized above the center of the table. Dawn let the visualization run until the small black creatures swarmed toward Joqi. Of course, the visualization didn't reveal the fear he felt during the daydream, and Dawn stopped the visualization before the creatures started eating Joqi's flesh.

Those in attendance showed various emotions, from shock to wonderment to disbelieving looks. The murmurs stilled and they waited for Joqi to continue.

"Dawn, show the information about the Clacs."

Dawn projected the image of a Clac above the table, and then summarized what was known about the species. The summary included the conclusion by those on Earth that the Clacs posed a future threat to human civilization—they were colonizing solar systems primarily in the direction of Earth's solar system. This prompted questioning of Eve and Dawn about the source and accuracy of their information.

After the discussion quieted down, High Priest Harsn spoke directly to Joqi's simulacrum. "Your revered grandfather had many visions that provided insights to guide us in preparing for the future we are currently in."

She paused and looked around at the others. "I am unsure what the message is for us from this dream, this vision of Joaquin's, but I am sure it is of great importance."

"I have given this some thought," Joqi injected before anyone else could speak. "My dream may have more importance regarding what we should do in general than it does regarding a threat specifically from the Clacs. Our long range scans have revealed no vessels of any kind near the intersection point."

"Please continue," the supreme leader said, cutting off others who had questions.

"I believe it means we should put in place resources to counter future aggressive threats to Zilia from space. This should start by assessing the range of threats considered possible, and then those considered most likely given our knowledge about other civilizations in our neighborhood of space. We should then put in place resources to counter the most likely threats."

"I find this most distasteful," the High Priest said. "Even so, we must take steps to protect our future generations."

"Thank you for sharing your dream," Ciasan Tojmera said. "I believe we all agree with your assessment. It will be difficult to prepare for a possible war, given that we have never been a warring civilization. We will discuss this and initiate appropriate actions."

The meeting was in effect over. Joqi's father requested a private discussion with him, and the others departed from the meeting, including Eve and Dawn.

"How is Mother holding up," Joqi asked. Among his blood kin, she was having the most difficulty with his departure.

"She is doing better. We all are, although our lives will never be the same." His father coughed, and then continued. "However, we do have some good news for you."

His father motioned toward the door.

Ecina! She rushed toward his simulacrum, and then stopped a few feet away, realizing how he was represented.

"Oh Joqi, I have missed you so much!"

"I have missed you as well," he replied, suddenly feeling guilty that his emotion wasn't as true as hers.

"Do you see a change in me," she asked demurely, twirling about.

He looked closer. No, not really. But then, she seemed very happy for a new wife talking to her husband that was placing considerably more distance between them with each passing second.

She stopped twirling and the words gushed from her mouth. "I am pregnant! You're going to be a father!"

Joqi was dumbstruck by this announcement, but recovered quickly. They had been married three and half months now, but had spent only a few nights together before he was immersed fulltime in the smart plasma aboard the *Horizon Quest*. He recalled with pleasure that they had slept very little those few nights.

"Sweetheart, this is wonderful!" Looking closer, he could see a slight plumpness around her waist.

His mother had joined his father, and both were smiling proudly.

"We are looking forward to a new grandbaby to spoil," his mother said, and his father nodded his agreement.

Joqi felt truly blessed. It was obvious how happy Ecina was with her condition.

Ecina wiped away some tears as her smile faltered. Joqi ached to hold her, and without thinking, focused intently on solidifying his simulacrum's hands. He moved close to Ecina and cupped her face in his tenuous grasp, eliciting a gasp of surprise and pleasure from her at his tender touch.

# CHAPTER 8

"**H**ow accurate must we be when crossing the intersection point?" Dawn asked.

Joqi hesitated before answering. He was sure his grandpapa knew they would have to accelerate all the way to the intersection point to get there in time. Even if they had left on the day he died, they would travel through the point at a significant velocity.

"Grandpapa said we must be at the intersection point at a specific time. I take that to mean exactly at the specified time and point."

"I agree," Dawn said. "At our current acceleration, we will arrive several hours before the specified time. We will need to adjust our acceleration as we get closer."

Joqi was lost in thought for a short time as he considered the importance of the extra line of intersection on the map his grandpapa gave him. Until now he had assumed the reference vector from Zilia's outer moon to the intersection point was provided to ensure the point was accurately determined. But there was another possible explanation.

"Another point we should address," he said reflectively, "is the vector of our path to the point including our intersection angle"

Dawn waited for him to continue.

"What if the fourth vector, the dashed one from our outer moon to the intersection point was meant to denote our line of approach to the point?"

This idea caused Dawn to pause before answering. "I can think of no rationale for this."

"Nor can I," he replied. "However, that approach vector is as good as any, if we can still adjust our trajectory to fit that vector."

Dawn remained quiet. From the calculations and trajectory curves appearing above the virtual control console, Joqi knew she was calculating the exact position of the approach vector based on where all the reference points, the outer moon included, would be positioned at the specified intersection time. Then Dawn replaced the calculations and trajectory curves with a 3-D visualization of the outer moon reference vector and the required *Horizon Quest's* trajectory to intersect with the reference vector.

"Thanks, Dawn. I understand we need to adjust our course quickly."

"I am doing so now, Commander."

He smiled at her abrupt reference to his command position aboard the *Horizon Quest.* He had learned how to control all the spaceship systems, including the propulsion systems. He had learned just as quickly that Dawn was much more adept than he was at controlling the flight of the *Horizon Quest*. He routinely deferred to her in navigation and spaceship control matters.

They needed to place all sensors in an optimal collection configuration as they approached the intersection point, but he would take care of that. He would also make sure all sensor data and internal ship systems data were recorded as they approached and passed through the intersection point.

Joqi quietly pondered another curious detail about the information his grandpapa had provided—the timing of their arrival at the intersection point. The specified time coincided exactly with the peak of the next Holy Seven-Year Two-Moon Eclipse as viewed from the Temple of Zilerip. This holiest of the primary two-moon eclipses occurred when the outer moon was closest to Zilia in its seven year elliptical orbit around the planet. This "Holy Seven-Year" eclipse peaked at the time of the vernal equinox on the planet, the first day of spring.

*So, what surprise will the first day of spring bring on Zilia this year*, he mused.

• • •

There was nothing at the intersection point they could see, absolutely nothing. They were going to cross it at precisely the time and vector angle specified in Prophet Sepeda's drawing. Joqi made sure they were streaming sensor data back to Zilia via Hycoms links. This included video focused on the intersection point as they approached it.

Joqi saw a shimmering mirror slit pop into existence an instant before the *Horizon Quest* reached the intersection point. Before he could assimilate anything else, the spaceship's pointed nose intersected the point, and the ship passed through the mirrored slit.

Joqi felt disoriented instantly, like his thoughts, his physical being, were disassociating from reality. His mind sensed a vast, dark nothingness, and then a confusing flow of images and data pressed in. Smeared, bright spirals and other illuminated images were visible in all directions, spread across a background of undulating black fabric. In addition, the ship sensors presented a wide range of electromagnet data, most of which was nonsensical. This in turn started slipping away, and he grasped for something to anchor himself to, something that would focus his thoughts and maintain the sanity he felt fading away like daylight rushing into darkness. He could sense a vast, dark firmament. Time meant nothing.

He focused on that special, personal place established in his mind when he went into deep meditation. It was the place his brother Rauli had taught him to go, a place where immersion in the smart plasma became a distant thought. He sat cross-legged on a floating velvet cushion in a sea of undulating blackness. Small pinpricks of light emerged randomly in the distance; the stars were calling to him.

One of the bright pinpricks coalesced into a sparkling light that drew nearer. The light morphed into the image of a fluttering butterfly; no, it looked more like an angel.

The angel in turn transformed to someone familiar. It was Ecina!

Ecina was dancing to an unheard song, like a little girl pirouetting to her own pretend music. By shear will power, Joqi closed the distance between them, and saw that she was wearing the same provocative outfit she wore on their last night together. The outfit shifted to a thin, long white gown that was just opaque enough to tease him with her semi-nudity. She stopped dancing and reached for him, her eyes shining with excitement. He laughed and ran to hold her, to pull her close. She felt different from before, and he pulled away; she was much larger around her waist. Their child!

Joqi pulled her close again and sensed her healthiness and her happiness at their forthcoming parenthood. They laughed and played and talked and loved. He was unconcerned about where he was or what might be going on elsewhere. He just wanted to live in this dream as long as he could.

Ecina pulled away and began dancing again, the thin gown highlighting her beauty and sensuality. She twirled and stepped to a tune only she could hear as she receded into shifting shadows. She dissolved rapidly and he sensed other data pressing for attention.

• • •

The *Horizon Quest's* sensors provided coherent data streams stimulating Joqi's interest. At first he was confused by the influx of raw data. He quickly regained focus and viewed a strange, panoramic, star studded firmament stretching in all directions. One star shined much brighter than all the others.

They must be near another solar system. Or were they? For all he knew they were still in some weird dimension accessed through the mirror slit at the intersection point. The thought that they had transitioned quickly to a distant solar system was mind boggling.

*Dawn?*

*Yes, Joaquin, I am here.*

That was a relief, to say the least. Dawn explained that she remembered the *Horizon Quest* thrusting into the intersection point, but in the next instant in her recollection, they entered the current region of space. Sensors that were set to start recording before crossing the intersection point showed incoherent noise from the time they crossed the point until they appeared in their current location.

Why could he sense things during the transition and Dawn was unable to? Had he seen and held Ecina during the transition? Or was it a waking dream as the *Quest* entered the current region of space? As fascinating as the transition anomaly was, he had to stop this introspection and join Dawn in assessing their situation.

Dawn pointed out their high velocity when crossing the intersection point was probably a critical factor in making the transition safely; the shimmering slit that opened in space-time was likely open for only a fraction of a second. There was no telling what would have happened if the *Horizon Quest* had not made it completely through the slit before it closed.

Sensor recordings started the instant they transitioned into the current region of space. This pinpointed the location and time of their arrival. Dawn verified that all sensor data recording was ongoing. She had already determined they were in the outer reaches of a solar system located some seventeen light-years from the star Eta Sagittarii, which was positioned on toward the center of the Sagittarius constellation. This meant they were about 118 light-years from Zilia. The local star shined brighter than the Zilan star Arzét. Its luminosity was about twenty percent more than that of Arzét.

Dawn's attempts to establish a Hycoms communication link with Zilia had failed, but she would keep trying so they could provide a status report and consult with those back home. Diagnostics on the Hycoms system showed no problems. Those back home were surely worried about the *Horizon Quest* disappearing.

The star field view was like nothing Joqi had ever seen or imagined. It took him several minutes to adjust to this view of the Milky Way galaxy, a view from a perspective never seen before by humans or their interstellar probes. To help resolve this perspective in his mind, he needed a reference point, the spot through which they came into this region of space.

A tracking spot came up on a virtual display, annotated with the *Horizon Quest's* velocity vector. It was scary how he only had to think something to have Dawn act on it. To say they were becoming close was a gross understatement.

Dawn added another reference point in the virtual display, showing the local star's position with respect to their current location. She then added two more points relatively close to their location, annotated as large outer planets orbiting the local star. These large planets could explain the scarcity of asteroids in the outer regions of the solar system; over time they had pulled most of the orbiting objects in, adding to their mass. However, several small objects were detected in toward the nearest planet. They could be asteroids or small moons. In addition, there was a thin band of asteroids located out past their point of entry at the outer edge of the solar system.

*We need more information fast,* Joqi projected. *We are fairly screaming into this solar system at a high relativistic velocity. Do we continue, or do we try to go into braking orbits around one or more of the large outer planets?*

*That is your call, Joaquin. I will continue to collect data about this system to help you make that decision.*

This statement gave Joqi pause; a circumspect response from Dawn was unusual.

His intuition was telling him this solar system must be their destination. They didn't have enough fuel to make it to another star system, nor did they have guidance information to another intersection point, a transition point. Whatever higher power guided their actions to arrive in this solar system was providing no further guidance!

Joqi initiated a full electromagnetic spectrum scan of the solar system, focusing on the area within forty-five degrees out from the local star. He was rewarded immediately with multiple signal detections coming from the inner region of the system. This solar system was occupied!

*This solar system is our destination,* Joqi conveyed. He was sure of it. *I am shutting down our propulsion engines to conserve fuel while we assess our situation.*

*I agree,* Dawn replied. *My location calculations and initial assessment of the EM signals indicates we are entering the home solar system of the crustacean-like alien creatures detected by Earth long ago.*

Joqi shivered at the memory of his dreams in which the miniature Clacs swarmed to eat him alive. He shook this off and accessed data taken from Earth archives about the Clac solar system. He projected this solar system layout in a virtual display alongside the solar system display Dawn was assimilating based on direct observations.

Earth's model showed the Clac star as being close to the same class as the sun in Earth's solar system, but a billion and a half years older and having a luminosity about fifteen percent more than Earth's sun. Earth's estimate of luminosity was low by about five percent. The aging Clac star was entering the transition stage toward eventually becoming a red giant star. More important for life in the Clac solar system, the local star's luminosity was nearing the tipping point of heating the inner planets to a level that would terminate all life on those planets.

Earth's model accounted for only one large outer object, a class L brown dwarf star. The model showed this massive object had grown to almost the mass necessary to jumpstart a fusion reaction in its core, just short of becoming a bright star. Zilan astronomers and scientists preferred calling such massive brown dwarfs as sub-stars to clearly differentiate them from active stars, which had nuclear fusion reactions ongoing in their cores. Brown dwarfs did not have fusion reactions ongoing, although they did radiate significant energy, mostly in infrared rays.

Joqi closed the display of Earth's model and concentrated on the actual solar system layout in Dawn's display, which now showed seven planets orbiting the local star, including the brown dwarf sub-star, which was the sixth large body out from the star. Dawn's model also showed a large object orbiting the brown dwarf, a large moon or planet.

The model showed the fourth planet out from the star was the only one in the habitable zone, that is, in the zone where temperatures on the planet supported formation of liquid water. This must be the Clac home world.

The large outermost planet and the brown dwarf appeared to orbit in sync around the local star. The brown dwarf was a smaller class T instead of the larger class L brown dwarf shown in Earth's model. It was likely that Earth detected the two outer objects as one huge object since the two were in synced orbits. The brown dwarf looked dark red with a deep blue halo around its rim. It had the appearance of a very old brown dwarf sub-star.

Joqi looked at the fourth planet through a high resolution telescopic sensor. The planet was well to the left and below the star in its orbit, and looked like a perfectly smooth dull pearl. There were two moons near the planet; one very large one and a small one farther out than the large one.

He focused the telescopic sensor to magnify the planet's image. High, pearly clouds hid the surface from view.

But here and there he could make out dark spots in the clouds, which were surely the tops of very high mountains. He recalled his vision at his grandpapa's deathbed of standing on a high mountain looking down on pearly white clouds and watching a very bright sun set at the horizon. This planet was where his grandpapa wanted him to go!

He turned his attention to the pressing issue of their next course of action. They were traveling too fast to go into orbit around the mid-region planets in this solar system, unless they first braked significantly using the *Horizon Quest's* engines. And traveling through half the solar system at a very high velocity to enter a braking orbit around the central star made him uneasy. They would consume most of their fuel reserve slowing down on the way to the star. And what would the Clacs make of it?

No, it would be best to use the *Horizon Quest's* engines and braking orbits around the large outer planet, and then the brown dwarf, to slow to a reasonable velocity for the inward journey to the Clac planet. Closer assessment of the sub-star revealed it had a thick atmosphere that extended inward toward its core. They would fly through the atmosphere of the outermost planet, and then move inward to a braking orbit in the massive brown dwarf's atmosphere.

Joqi smiled as he sensed the *Horizon Quest* flipping end-over-end to point its engines toward the outer planet. A trajectory to intercept the planet was highlighted on the solar system display. The spaceship's engines roared to life, starting the deceleration sequence. As usual, Dawn was following his thoughts and conclusions.

Dawn fine-tuned the braking trajectory and displayed the results. They would enter a partial orbit through the atmosphere of the nearby large planet to brake and vector the *Horizon Quest* to intercept the brown dwarf sub-star. They would make several braking orbits around the brown dwarf, dipping just inside its atmosphere, then slingshot the spaceship into a trajectory to intercept the Clac planet. This would conserve fuel for use in navigating into orbit around the Clac planet. It would also conserve enough fuel to navigate around the solar system as necessary.

*I am proceeding with your plan,* Dawn conveyed, just to make sure Joqi understood her actions. *I have calculated the trajectory to intersect with the closest planet. I will fine tune our trajectory as we get closer to the planet where I can better analyze using its atmosphere for braking.*

Once Dawn had the *Horizon Quest* in the proper trajectory toward the large outer planet, Joqi engaged her again in discussing the nature of the anomaly they passed through to get to the Clac solar system. The anomaly was nothing like he thought a wormhole would be, considering all the scientific speculation he was aware of on the nature of potential wormholes. They went over again all the recorded information from crossing the intersection point to finding themselves in the Clac solar system.

Joqi concluded they had either transitioned through a very short wormhole or through some kind of dimensional window between their entry and exit points. They had no firm data supporting either hypothesis. And with their Hycoms system inoperable, they had no way to consult with the scientists back on Zilia.

Dawn was following his ruminations. *Did you know your Grandfather had a problem with the Hycoms system on his ship, the* New Horizon, *when attempting to communicate messages to Earth about the* Third Moon Rising *miracle?*

*No,* Joqi replied. *What is the relevance of that to our Hycoms problem?*

*The failure caused Commander Sepeda to make decisions on his own regarding the significance of the event, which set him on the path to becoming Prophet Sepeda.*

*I'm no Prophet in the making,* Joqi conveyed. *But the Hycoms failure certainly means we are on our own in addressing forces encountered in this solar system.*

• • •

They had just entered a braking orbit around the brown dwarf, when Dawn indicated a distress signal was intercepted, apparently from a Clac spaceship. The Clac vessel was on the opposite side of the brown dwarf from the *Horizon Quest's* approach path, which blocked them from receiving the signal earlier.

Joqi didn't question Dawn's assessment that it was a distress signal; she had more than enough data in the pilfered Earth files to decipher the Clac spaceship's emergency transmission. He got busy assessing the information Dawn was presenting in virtual displays.

The Clac spaceship was in orbit around the large planet they had detected earlier orbiting the enormous brown dwarf. Dawn's data showed the planet had a very thin atmosphere. A full spectrum scan of the ship revealed it was emitting no coherent radiation other than the omni-directional distress signal. Clearly its propulsion system had been shut down for some time; otherwise they should see some level of infrared radiation. Either that or it had an ion, plasma, or other exotic propulsion system that gave off no radiation signature.

*How many braking orbits to slow us down enough to maneuver to the planet?*

Dawn took a few seconds before replying to Joqi's query.

*Three, if we go deeper into the atmosphere to get more friction. Twelve if we stay at our current orbital altitude in the upper atmosphere. I caution against reducing altitude. It would push our deceleration to over seven-g and black out most of our sensors.*

Dawn waited patiently for his decision. He could sense her unease, if you could call it that for an artificial intelligence entity. The brown dwarf's atmosphere was thick, mostly hydrogen and helium, and became soupy very fast at lower altitudes. And the sub-star's gravity increased dramatically as the altitude decreased.

*Take us lower, but keep us well above the three orbit altitude,* Joqi conveyed. *Modify our course to have us exit orbit in a direction and at a speed that will intercept the large planet.*

*Changing orbit now,* Dawn replied. *It will be a rough ride.*

Joqi could feel the sharp increase in drag and buffeting of the ship as Dawn took them deeper into the atmosphere of the giant brown dwarf. One mistake or propulsion problem now would plunge the *Horizon Quest* into the deep gravity well of the sub-star, quickly destroying the ship and all in it.

*I don't want to believe our path here was predestined,* Joqi thought reflectively. *However, everything that has happened to get us here sure lines up that way.*

Dawn gave no response. After seven orbits of the brown dwarf, she directed the *Horizon Quest* on a path to intercept the large planet and its captive Clac spaceship.

# PART 2

# CHAPTER 9

As Dawn piloted the *Horizon Quest* into orbit around the large planet, Joqi analyzed the information collected about the planet. It was larger and denser than their home world of Zilia. He estimated the gravity at the planet's surface was over three times what it was on the surface of Zilia. The planet always presented the same side to the brown dwarf, and that side was scorching hot from the infrared radiation from the brown dwarf sub-star. The other side was in deep freeze. It wasn't a place he wanted to visit.

Dawn displayed the estimated orbit of the Clac spaceship. It was an elliptical orbit around the planet, elongated toward the brown dwarf when between the planet and the brown dwarf. The spaceship's orbit skimmed close to the planet when on the opposite side away from the brown dwarf. The Clac spaceship would get closer to the large planet on each outbound leg of the orbit, a curious and soon fatal orbit.

*How many orbits before the Clac vessel crashes into the planet,* Joqi queried.

*I estimate no more than fifteen more orbits,* Dawn replied. *I am positioning the Horizon Quest to match the Clac ship orbit when it turns back toward the planet.*

Joqi focused full spectrum sensors to scan space around the brown dwarf and in toward the Clac home planet. He could detect no vessels anywhere near their region of space. Clearly there was no rescue attempt being made by the Clacs. Considering the degrading orbit of the nearby spaceship, he could understand why. Even having advanced propulsion engines, it was unlikely that a rescue ship could arrive in time to save the damaged vessel.

Dawn indicated that signals intercepted coming from the region of the Clac world revealed they planned another research expedition soon to the brown dwarf and its large planet. Whatever was driving them to survey the brown dwarf and its planet must be very important.

Joqi observed with approval as Dawn nudged the *Horizon Quest* into a matching orbit with the Clac ship, positioning them within 100 meters of the tumbling spaceship. She piloted the *Quest* with a finesse he had yet to master.

The Clac vessel was twirling end-over-end like a large two bladed fan revolving around its orbital path. Each rotation revealed a jagged hole in the back quarter-length of the vessel, near what was likely the propulsion system area. The hole stood out in stark relief from the smooth black hull of the alien ship. The jagged sides of the hole were bent inward, evidence of an object striking the ship. Continued observations revealed no exit hole for whatever had hit the Clac ship.

*The damage was likely caused by a small asteroid,* Dawn observed.

*This is surprising,* Joqi replied. *Our scans showed space near the brown dwarf clear of asteroids.*

He scrutinized images taken earlier of the planet's surface. There was indeed evidence of recent impacts of small asteroids. The brown dwarf did a good job of sweeping space clean near its orbital path. But the small craters on the planet's surface indicated there were still some infrequent, long period asteroid showers coming from somewhere.

Joqi initiated another full spectrum scan of the Clac vessel. Earlier scans had shown the only radiation coming from the vessel was the emergency beacon. This scan showed no sign of activity or life aboard the ship. There was no question that the Clac ship was dead in space.

• • •

It took seven orbits of the large planet to stop the Clac vessel's tumbling. They stopped the end-over-end tumbling by sending a team of propulsion capable, shape-shifting robots to push against the spaceship's hull at appropriate points. Dawn then positioned the *Horizon Quest* within fifty meters of the damaged vessel and aligned with it front to back.

Joqi took direct control of one of the robots, making it an extension of him. He could see and sense everything the robot could. He guided the robot through the jagged hole in the hull and into the first narrow, tunnel-like passageway leading toward the front of the ship. The robot had to change shape to lower its height to navigate the narrow passageway. A quick check of the robot's sensors indicated no radiation was coming from inside the ship.

The robot began a damage assessment and search of the ship. It came upon a Clac a short distance down the narrow passageway. It was pinned under a large metal beam near where the intruding asteroid had broken through the thick outer hull. To all appearances, the Clac was dead, but Joqi still felt rising panic while viewing it at close range through the robot's sensors. Would the fear induced by his dreams about the Clac hoard swarming toward him ever go away!

Steeling himself, Joqi maneuvered his robot host closer to the alien. The large beam had smashed into the Clac's hindquarters, cutting deep into its body. A thick, brown colored substance had oozed from the wound and solidified from exposure to the cold vacuum of space. The alien wore no protective suit or any other equipment to keep it alive in the exposed passageway. There was no way the creature could be alive.

He started to turn the robot to continue searching the ship, but stopped when he detected a small quiver in one of the front appendages of the creature. Or was it his imagination working overtime? He played back the visual sensor data and confirmed the appendage had moved. The alien was alive, but just barely. How could it survive for no telling how long in the vacuum of space?

*The Clac's are oxygen breathers,* Dawn conveyed, *but can go for long periods without breathing. Apparently it goes dormant in an emergency like this, which is why our sensors did not pick up any sign of life on the vessel.*

Joqi turned the robot to look more closely at the passageway. Alien tools were scattered nearby. They were probably magnetized in some fashion, for they all stuck to the metal corridor here and there. It appeared the Clac had started clearing debris when the beam smashed into it.

He turned the robot back to view the Clac. His robot could lift the beam from the alien, but how could it tend to the creature while holding the beam. He needed another robot to help...or he could go there himself!

*No Joaquin. You must stay aboard the* Horizon Quest. *It is too dangerous to leave!*

Dawn's appeal notwithstanding, Joqi knew he must go help the Clac. His intuition was telling him he must face his fear now. It was also time to test his ability to exit the smart plasma after being immersed for so long. He had practiced meditation the way his brother had advised him to do; hopefully that would enable him to function outside the smart plasma with manageable side effects.

The access hatch to the command pod slid back noiselessly. Joqi lay in the smart plasma trying to follow through on his decision to go to the Clac spaceship. It took all his willpower to stand up and break free of the plasma. The plasma slowly receded from his upper torso, as if clinging on to the one reason for its existence. He was just as reluctant to leave the plasma, but with a surge of resolve, he climbed out of the command pod and stood on the access platform until the last of the plasma receded into the pod. He was thankful for the light gravity maintained in the pod compartment; it helped steady him physically.

He retrieved underclothing and a spacesuit from a locker, and then went to find a ride to the Clac vessel. Dawn had a utility pack waiting for him at the airlock chamber, and cautioned him to turn on the suit electromagnetic bubble shield during transit. She had detected high levels of cosmic radiation in this region of space, and the shield would protect against most of the radiation during his transit.

Joqi felt more uneasy the farther he rode in an exoskeleton robot away from the *Horizon Quest*. Granted, it was a short fifty meter ride to the Clac vessel, but it seemed like an eternity to him. He felt a gnawing emptiness growing inside that could only be filled by direct contact with the smart plasma. The yawning vastness of space viewed through his spacesuit visor wasn't helping matters any, nor did the view of the huge brown dwarf close by. He focused intently on the alien spaceship just a short distant away, shutting out other distracting thoughts and observations.

Once inside the alien vessel, Joqi's nerves settled down somewhat. He activated the electromagnetic function in the exoskeleton's feet so he could crouch and walk along the passageway. He made his way cautiously down the narrow tunnel to where the Clac was pinned under the beam. He was thankful for his exoskeleton robot's ability to maneuver in zero gravity environments.

The robot he had left at the scene was waiting beside the Clac. Joqi had studied images of Clacs obtained from data Dawn imported from Earth's data files, but he was ill prepared for what he was viewing in the close quarters of the narrow passageway. He found the alien repugnant, and not just visually. His suit sensors indicated the creature was outgassing an awful stench. He shuddered at the memory of the much smaller alien creatures swarming to bite into his flesh.

The Clac's torso was oval shaped, with the front end slightly larger than the backend. He recognized the Clacs visual sensors, its eyes, at the ends of four vertical stalks equally spaced along the front end of the torso above its two mandibles. The Clac's four leg appendages along each side of its stretched oval body were covered by wiry hair-like whiskers. Two short pincher appendages, or mandibles, extended out below the visual sensors and just above a horizontal slit that must be its mouth.

Joqi shook his head vigorously, trying to shake off the growing sense of urgency to return to immersion in the smart plasma pod. He must focus on the injuries the Clac had suffered!

The metal beam had slashed deep into the Clac's back, pinning it against the inner wall. With the zero gravity in the passageway, the beam must have been loaded with spring tension for it to break free and cut into the Clac. Joqi noticed a thin line running from one of the Clac's back legs to a stanchion tie point down the passageway. The alien was protecting itself from floating into the large gash in the ship's hull and on into space. But why did the Clac venture into the passageway with no visible life support?

The Clac lay perfectly still, showing no sign of life. But then, Joqi was unsure about what a Clac would show in way of vital signs if it were alive. Surely the visual sensors or some of the appendages would be moving if it were still alive. There was dry, light brown material spread out along the Clac's back from the wound area.

He steeled himself and moved closer to the alien. He used a medical scanner from his utility pack to methodically scan the Clac's entire body, with the scan data transmitted simultaneously to the *Horizon Quest*. He carefully avoided touching the carcass while doing the scan.

But Joqi could see no way to help the alien without touching it, so he squatted and reached toward the middle of the alien's back. He couldn't make himself touch it on his first attempt, even though he was protected by his suit gloves. He tried again, and this time pressed down in the middle of the Clac's back to hold it firmly against the passageway inner wall. The alien's hard shell back looked smooth, but had a texture like fine sandpaper.

Joqi directed the first robot on the scene to lift the beam off the Clac. The alien jerked uncontrollably as the beam was removed, and then the jerking quickly subsided. A fresh mucous-like material, dark brown this time, began oozing from the wound. The mucous started solidifying in the cold vacuum of the passageway. Joqi quickly pulled gauze and tape from his medical kit while leaning against the alien to hold it in place. He bandaged the wound area as best he could.

*What now,* he wondered. The Clac remained motionless.

Joqi shined a light down the passageway; he was thankful Dawn had outfitted his utility pack to meet most contingencies. He saw a closed hatch several meters beyond the nearby stanchion. In the zero gravity, it was easy to pull the Clac along to the hatch. He got a good look at the bottom of the creature's body for the first time. It was slightly rounded, side-to-side, and had four shell sections overlapping from front to back. Jointed leg appendages extruded out from the sides of each section. Each appendage had a formidable looking claw section at its end

Joqi operated a manual release on the hatch and almost lost grip on the alien when pressurized gas slammed the released hatch into the exoskeleton robot. He pulled the Clac through the hatch and closed it, a feat impossible for him to achieve without the added strength of the exoskeleton.

Apparently the ship had a backup power system, for the pressure in the passageway began increasing. He pulled the alien along with him to the next hatch, and waited for the gas pressure in the passageway to stabilize. An analysis of the gas showed it was comprised of oxygen, hydrogen, helium, nitrogen and traces of other elements. The oxygen level was lower than he was used to, but he could survive breathing for short periods in the gas if necessary. The high level of helium would affect his vocal cords, making his voice come out high pitched.

*This is fascinating,* Dawn projected as Joqi continued along the passageway, pulling the Clac through hatch after hatch. *The Clac has what looks like nine small brains, one inward from each leg and one behind and above the eye stalks.*

Joqi stopped in his tracks with the Clac floating behind him.

*You've kidding,* he said. *Are you sure they are brain modules? Couldn't they be muscles to operate the legs?*

*I am sure,* Dawn declared firmly.

*Hmmm, does that make them geniuses?*

*It depends,* Dawn conveyed. *Each of the brains is smaller than ours. But all together, they are much larger than ours. The level of intelligence will depend on how the brains are wired and how much of each brain is actually used. A large percentage of the brains capacity may be for information storage. We have to wait until we can collect more information to understand their capabilities.*

Joqi didn't reply. They had a lot to figure out. He continued pulling the Clac down the passageway until they entered what looked like a command and control center. He anchored the Clac to the floor in back of the compartment using tape from the medical kit. He moved back and stepped out of the exoskeleton. His boots were lightly magnetized, enabling him to walk slowly on metal surfaces.

Dawn had insisted he bring a wide variety of devices on the sortie, and the utility pack was full. One device was a portable communication system that also had an integrated translator, which was programmed per Earth's data for translating the Clac language. It could also project a 3-D image of whoever was communicating from back on the *Horizon Quest.* Joqi placed the device on the back bulkhead where it could project the image out about two meters from the wall, and then activated the device.

"So there you are," Dawn said through the communicator. Her comment verified the device was working, which was her intent. She projected a 3-D test image of Joqi into the compartment.

"This control center looks undamaged," Joqi said, looking around. "See what you can determine about the controls."

"In progress," Dawn replied.

Joqi examined the Clac again. Dark brown fluid was now oozing through the bandage he had placed over the gash in the Clac's back. A better compression bandage was needed to stem the flow from the gash.

He retrieved bandages and tape from the robot's storage compartment, and turned back toward the alien. He was reaching to take off the soaked bandage when the Clac's appendages started twitching, followed by its four stalk eyes opening. Joqi held his breath as the stalks moved, apparently giving the alien a view of its surroundings. Then the deep black orbs focused intently on Joqi, sending chills of apprehension through him.

In the next instant, the Clac pinned Joqi on his back on the metal deck. Joqi wanted to scream as he looked at the bottomless, black orbs staring at him as the Clac raised one pincher tipped leg in a menacing manner. The alien hesitated, and then turned two eye stalks to look over its back. It then looked at the bandage material Joqi still held.

The creature reared up and skittered backwards away from Joqi, trailing the medical tape he had used to attach it to the floor. The Clac bumped against the back bulkhead and stood there quivering. It turned two of its eye stalks to look over its back again at Joqi's hasty attempt to bandage the gash.

All the alien's visual receptors focused again fully on Joqi, and he reacted by moving as quickly as he could back into the exoskeleton. His quick movement caused the alien to skitter forward about a meter. The creature began emitting high frequency squeaks and clicks.

*Use the translator,* Dawn suggested sharply.

Joqi took several deep breaths, trying to calm down. His quick retreat to the safety of the exoskeleton robot was spontaneous. He must overcome this deep rooted fear!

Joqi linked with the translator, and said, "I mean you no harm."

This caused the Clac to stop all activity. It stood silently on all appendages, apparently trying to understand what Joqi was saying.

"Apogee...apogee," squeaked the translator.

What the heck? Apogee was a term describing a point in an objects orbit. Was the Clac concerned about its spacecraft crashing into the planet?

The translator squawked again, "Apology...apology."

Did the alien want him to apologize? But apologize for what? Clearly the translator algorithms obtained from Earth's archives needed updating to more accurately translate the Clac language.

"Apologize...you helped!" the Clac said, shuffling nervously again.

*Do I apologize,* Joqi thought. *No, it's apologizing.*

"What will help?" Joqi conveyed via his translator.

"Will ... repair," the Clac said. "Need ... rest."

After a moment, it added, "What ... you?"

Joqi was sure a lot was being lost in the translations using Earth's algorithms. That was something they must work on, but later.

"I am Joaquin, a human."

After a long pause, the Clac said, "I ... Cssyza ... *szswn*"

"Cssyza," Joqi said, trying to repeat what he assumed the Clac's name was. He had no idea what *szswn* meant, unless it was its species. His translator pronounced the Clac's name as "Sissy-za" and its last word as "zwin", all one syllable.

To further answer the question about what he was, Joqi stepped out of the exoskeleton and began removing his spacesuit. Once stripped, except for light undershorts and magnetic shoes, he walked closer to the alien to let it examine him. The alien indeed gave off a rotten odor, but not as bad as he had expected. He smiled as he turned completely around, remembering the viewing custom he and Ecina performed before they were married.

The air in the compartment was acrid, and it became more difficult for him to breathe as the seconds ticked by.

Apparently Cssyza's inspection was complete, for it slumped to the floor. Joqi quickly donned his spacesuit, and then took several deep breaths to clear his lungs and satisfy his need for more oxygen. He retrieved the floating bandage material and tape, and proceeded to apply a new compression bandage on the alien's back. It remained still throughout the process.

After Joqi applied the bandage, Cssyza rose and walked up the back bulkhead to a row of cabinets. It opened one cabinet and retrieved a clear container full of small round lavender balls. It took out several and swallowed them, and brought the container back down to the deck. Joqi suspected the balls were some kind of medicine, perhaps like antibiotics the Zilans used to clear up infections.

Joqi was impressed with the agility of the injured *szswn* and its ability to walk up the metal bulkhead. The alien apparently had some kind of gripping mechanisms at the wrist joints just above the leg appendage claws.

He communicated with Cssyza to see if anything else could be done, but it again reiterated it needed rest. Joqi explained the terminal orbit the alien's vessel was in around the large planet, as best he could. Cssyza indicated it understood the situation, but refused to relocate to the *Horizon Quest* as Joqi suggested.

Joqi sensed something like shame when the *szswn* communicated its understanding of the situation. For some reason it preferred staying aboard its ship, even if that meant certain death. Perhaps letting its ship get into this dire situation would be viewed very unfavorably by those back on its home world.

After a tedious communication session, Joqi got Cssyza's okay to use robots to install a temporary patch over the hole in the external hull. This would enable pressurizing the hull to facilitate future internal repairs. It meant that entry and exit from the ship would be through the ship's airlock chamber.

When Joqi prepared to leave, Cssyza tapped a claw on the metal floor to get his attention.

"You...affect...Cssyza." The alien shifted nervously on its eight legs. "You...affect...me."

"What do you mean, affect?"

The alien slumped to the floor and closed its four eyes. As far as he could tell, it was in a dormant state much like the condition it was in when pinned under the metal beam.

Puzzled and unsure what else to do, Joqi turned and walked out of the compartment in his exoskeleton robot. On the way back to the *Horizon Quest*, he wondered if Cssyza was a male or female of its species. That was a question that could wait until they knew each other better.

Right now he desperately needed to get back into the smart plasma pod.

# CHAPTER 10

*I need access to the* szswn *ship specifications,* Dawn conveyed. *Or we need Cssyza to identify hull points where we can safely attach pushing struts.*

Dawn's pressing message pulled Joqi's thoughts out of a plasma induced meditation. He agreed with Dawn. They needed to act fast; the damaged ship would crash into the planet in another five orbits.

Dawn had calculated the center of mass of the alien's vessel. She accomplished this by observing the initial tumbling of the vessel when encountered in orbit around the large planet, plus measuring the amount of force the propulsion robots had exerted to stop the vessel's tumbling.

She displayed a 3-D model of the vessel with a transparent hull, showing her estimation of the vessel's internal structure based on several scans of the ship. The center of gravity was highlighted just forward of the engine room, along the centerline of the vessel running front to back. Dawn indicated the engine configuration was probably that of an advanced ion-drive propulsion system.

Joqi transmitted the 3-D model to Cssyza, and expressed the urgent need to identify pressure points on the spaceship's external hull they could use to push the ship safely away from the planet. He indicated points near the tail of the ship would be best. They could then use those points to more easily accelerate the ship into a trajectory back toward Cssyza's home world. Towing the ship was an impractical option in the near term; pushing it was the best approach considering their time and resource constraints.

Cssyza was a quick study and understood the urgency. It verified the location of the ships center of gravity, and identified points along and around the back half of the ship that represented major structural strength. That was good enough to support nudging the ship out of orbit around the planet. They would have time later to work out just how much force those points could withstand. And considering the large gap in understanding each other's language, time was what they needed.

Dawn deployed most of their reconfigurable robots to attach to the damaged ship's external hull in a strut configuration that could cradle the nose of the *Horizon Quest*. Joqi wasn't too keen on this approach. If the structure failed, they could damage all or most of their robots. But with their time constraint and lack of large structural beams to work with, it was the best approach. It was fortunate that the ship was a medium sized survey vessel, or they would have to consider more drastic measures, including rescuing Cssyza against its will and letting its ship crash into the planet.

*I detect several asteroids approaching our orbital path,* Dawn conveyed with a sense of urgency. *They must be associated with the one that damaged the alien's ship.*

*Great, that is all we need now,* Joqi replied. The asteroids were likely now captured in orbit around the brown dwarf. *Have the robots go to the opposite side of the* szswn *ship away from the asteroids.*

*I have done so,* Dawn replied. *The track of the asteroids reveals that three are of primary concern to us.*

*Can our high power lasers deflect them?*

*No, they are closing on us too fast,* Dawn said. *However, the lasers can disrupt them.*

He knew what she meant; disrupt like in pulverizing them. He didn't like revealing their laser capabilities to the *szswn,* but there wasn't much choice.

*Position the ship to track and disrupt them,* he commanded.

Dawn did so, resulting in only dust and small fragments of the disrupted asteroids hitting the ships. Joqi scanned and analyzed the asteroid dust and was surprised at the high metallic content in it.

Looking again at the damage to the *szswn* ship, he had another concern. They didn't need a surprise from a faster asteroid that could hit the *Horizon Quest* before they could detect and destroy the asteroid.

*We need to program our sensor control systems to automatically detect very fast incoming threat objects and fire the lasers automatically to destroy them.*

*That capability exists,* Dawn replied. *I will set the timing and object description parameters and activate the automatic control system.*

*Good. But be careful setting the descriptor parameters. We don't need to shoot any of our flying robots down.* Joqi smiled when Dawn didn't respond. She surely understood that he was joking, but so far he had never known her to include any humor in her speech or actions.

Dawn directed the robots to continue their task of building the strut assembly. The robots worked quickly as a team and configured their bodies into the desired structure at the backend of the *szswn* spaceship. Per Dawn's direction, the robots avoided attaching to points in the engine exhaust area. Dawn eased the *Horizon Quest* in behind the ship, and then moved the *Quest* forward to nestle in the strut assembly, much as it had in the strut harness of the Sayer Research Station orbiting Zilia.

On the next orbit segment as they turned back toward the large planet, they pushed the spaceship out of orbit and toward the *szswn's* home world.

• • •

The massive brown dwarf and its orbiting planet receded quickly into the background as the *Horizon Quest* pushed and accelerated the *szswn* vessel into a trajectory to intersect its home world. Cssyza indicated early on that it had reestablished communication with its mission controllers. They first expressed shock and bewilderment at the turn of events. Having their survey vessel and pilot rescued was appreciated. Having it done by humans was not. And as best Joqi could interpret, they were fearful about what this might mean for their future.

While Dawn focused on accelerating the two spaceships along the necessary trajectory to intersect Cssyza's home world's orbit, Joqi stayed busy interacting with Cssyza, gaining a better understanding of it and its language.

Early in their interaction, Cssyza asked Joqi how many humans were onboard his spaceship. Startled, he almost said one other, Dawn. He thought about it for a few seconds, and had a better idea, at least for the near term. He told Cssyza he was the only human onboard, but that his spaceship was an intelligent, self-aware entity in its own right, one that operated all systems as Joqi directed.

He could tell this was a difficult concept for the *szswn* to comprehend. Cssyza asked if the robots were also self-aware entities, and Joqi said no. He explained they were self-organizing extensions of the spaceship, or of himself when needed, like the exoskeleton he rode over to the *szswn* ship. This seemed to mollify Cssyza for the time being.

After Dawn was satisfied the two ships were on the right flight path to intercept the home world, Joqi asked her to conduct a detailed study of the solar system. He had the uneasy feeling a time would come when they would need to know much more precisely the details of this solar system.

Dawn agreed, and conveyed, *I have initiated the study.*

She paused, then added, *Joaquin, I know the stress you felt when out of the smart plasma. You need to meditate frequently like your brother suggested, building up your tolerance for being out of the plasma.*

Implied in her statement was the assumption he would need to spend time out of the plasma to interface with other *szswns* when they arrived at their world. Joqi agreed, and thanked her, before turning his attention back to understanding Cssyza and the *szswn* species.

Cssyza's comment about him "affecting" it puzzled Joqi for some time. But each time he brought up the topic, Cssyza diverted the conversation to another topic. The *szswn* insisted that most of their interaction be via communication links, not in person. This was okay with Joqi at first; he had no desire to leave the smart plasma command pod. And for all practical purposes, visiting Cssyza while in a spacesuit was no better than interacting via video. Nor did he savor additional direct interaction with the alien, for it brought fearful unease to the forefront of his thoughts.

Why was it so difficult to communicate with the *szswn*? Why were those on Earth never able to fully decipher the Clac language? Joqi reviewed the videos they had collected of his conversations with Cssyza. He reviewed again and again the recordings of his first few encounters with the *szswn*.

He noticed that Cssyza shuffled its front legs a little when talking. He halted the 3-D video under review and restarted it from the beginning. Yes, the front legs shuffled a little as the *szswn* talked. And the two mandibles moved as well, in a rhythm similar to that of the front legs.

He realized the *szswn* language was much more complex than anyone had imagined. It was a combination of leg/mandible sign language in sync with audible expression. A communication dance that provided flourish and continuity to the *szswn* language!

*I believe you are right,* Dawn conveyed. *Such insight—a language dance!*

*We must learn this dance,* Joqi replied.

Both Dawn and Joqi closely examined the videos of his interaction with Cssyza. From the observed "cause and effect" interactions, they documented many basic steps in the *szswn* language dance involving front leg and mandible movements. The mandibles were more expressive than the legs, which seemed to provide the flourish to the language.

Interaction with Cssyza improved greatly when Joqi added basic speech mannerisms by movement of his feet and arms, mimicking the movements of the *szswn's* front legs and mandibles when communicating. In addition, he discovered Cssyza had a small, cream colored panel of skin just under its mouth slit that vibrated at different frequencies when it spoke. The frequencies were just above the spectrum of human hearing.

Joqi had a fabricator robot build a panel for his translator that could receive and transmit the frequency components synchronized with the other speech elements. Dawn reprogrammed the translator to include adaptive algorithms to interpret the *szswn's* spoken language, which, with Joqi's use of sign language, richly enhanced communication with Cssyza.

Cssyza expressed its pleasure at the extent Joqi went to understand the *szswn* language elements. It became very cooperative and proactive in teaching its language to Joqi. He quickly learned more gestures, adding a comprehensive sign language element to their conversations. He and Dawn were correct in assuming the leg movements provided flourish to the *szswn* language, much as hand movements did for human languages. And the added translator panel rounded out Joqi's communication capability.

Once Joqi was confident in his ability to communicate fully with Cssyza, he asked several question about the *szswn* species, their history, and conditions on their home world. After some subtle prodding and offering information about his own people, Joqi managed to get Cssyza to provide general information about its species. It became clear that Cssyza still felt deeply indebted to him for freeing it from the damaged ship. He and Dawn saved Cssyza from certain death.

As Cssyza explained, the *szswns* were driven to develop space travel capability by the impending demise of their local star. The star had increased its luminosity significantly over the past 1,000 years, driving temperatures up significantly on the *szswn* species home planet. The exact time when the star would expand rapidly before imploding was unknown, but they knew it wasn't too far in the future. They knew all life on their world would die before the star expanded very much more. The star's increasing luminosity would heat the planet's atmosphere and surface to temperatures that would eliminate all life on the planet.

The *szswns* had closely monitored changes in their star for over 2,000 of their years, or about 1,600 Zilan years. More recently, they achieved spaceflight within their solar system, starting about 700 years in the past. They hoped it would provide an avenue of escape for enough of their young ones to ensure the survival of their species among the stars. They began a search in earnest for evidence of other habitable planets around stars reachable with "generation ships".

The *szswn* generation ship concept was similar to what Joqi had learned about the generation ships sent by Earth over 200 years earlier to colonize the planet Hope. Those aboard generation ships made the trip awake, in close knit communities living half-way normal lives. The ships from Earth had enough supplies to support up to three generations of colonists, if need be.

In their search for habitable planets, the *szswns* discovered electromagnetic emissions from a faraway planet, indicating the presence of other higher intelligence life-forms in their neighborhood of space. This planet was Earth, located some 140 light-years from the *szswns'* solar system. This prompted a more widespread search for other solar systems hosting advanced life-forms, and they discovered the planet Zilia, which also had resident advanced humanoids.

The *szswns* also discovered the planet Hope, which had a biosphere that could support life, but they detected no emissions attributable to higher life-forms. Considering the time it took for signals to travel from Hope to this solar system, the *szswns* should detect signals from there in the near future, if they were still monitoring that region of space.

Joqi told Cssyza his home world was Zilia, but stopped short of revealing that his grandfather was born on the planet Hope. He was surprised the *szswn* had not asked about his origin already. He provided a brief overview of conditions and society on Zilia, hoping to elicit more information from Cssyza about its home world.

Cssyza made a very intriguing observation. The *szswn* found it curious that three planets in close proximity, cosmologically speaking, would have similar life-forms. And two of the planets hosted similar intelligent humanoids. It seemed logical to the *szswn* that life-forms from one planet were taken to the other two worlds to seed life there.

Joqi agreed that it was curious. He had, in fact, researched this when going through advanced studies on Zilia. He refrained from telling Cssyza the third planet, Hope, now had resident humans as well. He also withheld information on the other human colonized world, New Earth.

Discovery of other advanced life-forms threw the *szswns*' leadership into a state of confusion and conflict, and shortly after that, the general population as well. They had long believed they were the only sentient beings in the universe. This reaction was similar to what the Zilans went through when first contacted by humans of Earth descent—those of the diplomatic team led by Joqi's grandfather, Carlos Sepeda.

After much turmoil and several changes in leadership, the decision was made to send generation ships to two solar systems that were reachable within the average lifetime of a *szswn*. Those selected for the emigration were expected to procreate another generation of *szswns* once at their destination. The goal was to have enough adults survive the journey to seed colonies in the two solar systems. It was coincidental, or so Cssyza claimed, that the two solar systems were in the general direction of Earth.

A *szswn* generation ship's maximum velocity was still at low relativistic speeds. But a *szswn* lived on average about three times as long as a human did. Travel to the nearest habitable planet took 132 *szswn* years, and the next habitable planet beyond that took an additional eighty-seven years, well within the lifespan of a *szswn*.

Joqi was duly impressed at the *szswns'* long term commitment to this project. But then, survival of the species was at stake. He told Cssyza how impressed he was with their effort to colonize other planets, and this elicited no noticeable change in the *szswn's* demeanor.

Cssyza turned to summarizing current conditions on its home world. The atmosphere was very acrid and uncomfortable for even a *szswn* to breathe. Most stayed in underground or enclosed structures where airborne pollutants were filtered out. The *szswns* still came out to celebrate major events from their past, and to perform certain functions that were best accomplished in the open.

The surface temperature was warm to hot, heated by the brightening local star. The *szswns* were experiencing a "hothouse" effect of sorts as suspended particles in the atmosphere from active volcanoes absorbed radiation.

The planet was half again as large as Zilia, and through back and forth discussion with Cssyza, Joqi estimated he would weigh approximately forty percent more on the planet's surface than he did on Zilia. Walking on the planet would be manageable for him for short distances, but he would tire very quickly. It would be best for him to go to the surface inside an exoskeleton robot if he had to go there.

The *szswns'* planet orbited its sun closer and faster than Joqi's home world of Zilia did around its sun. A hundred cycles, or years, on the planet was approximately eighty-two years on Zilia. The planet had a sizeable moon in close orbit around it. This resulted in very high, rapidly changing tides in large bodies of water. A smaller outer moon had little tidal effects.

A greater concern than the higher gravity on the planet was the low oxygen level in the air, even though atmospheric pressure was considerably higher than on Zilia. This, coupled with the very acrid nature of the air, meant Joqi needed to stay in his spacesuit on the surface and only take it off if an emergency situation dictated he do so.

Joqi asked Cssyza why the *szswns* were interested in the brown dwarf sub-star. Cssyza indicated that was something it would have to wait to answer.

He discovered there was one topic that was apparently taboo when talking to a *szswn*. Cssyza became unresponsive for several days when Joqi broached the topic of gender relationships in the *szswn* species. All attempts at communication went unanswered by Cssyza for several sleep periods, which prompted Joqi to suit up for another trip to check on the alien.

He sent a message to Cssyza indicating he was coming over because he was concerned about the *szswn's* health. There was no response from Cssyza, which caused Joqi to head over with some urgency.

He rode an exoskeleton robot like he had the first time, and had no trouble entering the *szswn* vessel through the airlock chamber. To his surprise, he found Cssyza waiting for him in the passageway outside the chamber.

"You must go back to your ship," Cssyza said emphatically.

"When you stopped communicating, I concluded something was wrong," Joqi replied.

Cssyza stared stoically at Joqi without replying. Joqi stood silently, staring unwaveringly at the *szswn's* four eyes. After several minutes, the *szswn* began shuffling its feet nervously.

"You affect me," Cssyza finally said. "Something I not explain."

"I mean you no harm, no ill will," Joqi said.

"I know," it said. "I feel…closeness with you after our many talks."

"And I with you," Joqi replied.

Cssyza stopped shuffling its feet and seemed to have reached an important decision, if Joqi was indeed reading its expressions correctly.

"You are here so must make most of it," Cssyza said. "My leaders have requested communication with you and me in same compartment."

Joqi smiled. Perhaps the leaders needed direct assurance that Cssyza had indeed encountered a human.

"That is okay with me. It is about time I introduced myself."

Cssyza turned and headed toward the ship's command center and Joqi followed. Once there, the *szswn* explained how the meeting would be conducted. The *szswns* used two dimensional displays for video communications; 3-D visualization used too much signal bandwidth and provided little additional content over 2-D communication. Besides, 3-D visualization systems had many more components that could fail.

Cssyza counseled Joqi next on how to interact with the *szswn* leaders. First, he should show deference to the leaders. They were prone to react strongly, and negatively, when confronted. Second, he must refrain from asking to meet with the leaders; he should wait for an invitation. Third, when asked what he was doing in this region of space, he should indicate he was on an exploratory mission to the brown dwarf and was surprised to discover a *szswn* vessel in distress there. And fourth, he must go through the session in person, outside his spacesuit.

*Well I'll be a saszu's uncle,* Joqi thought. *Dawn, are you following this?*

*Yes, and I recommend you do as Cssyza says. It is clearly trying to protect you and get you a meeting with its leaders, as you want.*

Yes, come to think of it, he did want a meeting. He realized that was what coming here was all about. He didn't know what he would say or do in the meeting, but the *szswns* emigration to planets located toward Earth had the makings of a serious future threat to humankind.

*I'll have difficulty breathing in this acrid environment,* Joqi conveyed.

*There are nose filters in your utility pack that will filter the air,* Dawn replied. *Breathe through your nose as much as possible. Breathe through your mouth only as required to communicate.*

*From what Cssyza says, you should remain silent most of the time. Get back in your spacesuit as soon as you can. The environment there has a lower level of oxygen than you are accustomed to.*

There was no need to answer Dawn; he agreed with her assessment.

"I will do as you say," Joqi said to Cssyza. "I need to wear my translator on my waist belt if I am to fully embrace the Clac language."

"That is acceptable," Cssyza said. "That will impress."

Joqi got out of his spacesuit as gracefully as he could, and retrieved the nose filters from the utility pack. They fit perfectly when he pushed one into each nostril. He should have known Dawn would provide what he needed for this eventuality.

"I am ready," he said. Then he had another thought. "What if they don't invite me to come meet them?"

"They will," Cssyza replied, with what Joqi thought was a humorous tone. "It is not every cycle that a human enters our solar system and rescues one of our valuable spaceships."

# CHAPTER 11

The large display screen showed two *szswns* perched atop an illuminated, raised circular platform in an otherwise darkened chamber. One was much larger than the other. The smaller *szswn* was positioned back a little from the large one. Joqi thought he saw some movement in the shadows around the platform, but he wasn't sure.

Apparently there was an established protocol for addressing the leaders. Cssyza made introductions, always addressing the large *szswn* while postured with its frontend lower than its backend. Kneeling, that was what it looked like to Joqi. To show his deference, as Cssyza suggested, Joqi squatted with one knee on the floor and his hands on the other knee. He bowed his head awaiting a cue that he should rise and address the two *szswns*. It was a bit galling to do this, considering he felt no real deference to the *szswns*, plus he and Dawn had rescued Cssyza and its ship.

Cssyza summarized the circumstances of its spaceship being hit by an asteroid while surveying the large planet orbiting the huge brown dwarf. The *szswn* next explained how the human and its spaceship had rescued the damaged ship. Cssyza wrapped up the summary by explaining the human, Joaquin, had made good progress in learning the *szswn* language.

Joqi waited patiently for Cssyza to complete the obligatory introductory report. No doubt the leaders already knew much more about him than he did about them.

"Rise, human," the large *szswn* finally said. Cssyza had addressed the leader as "Honored Pazrs, Exalted *Szswn* Leader".

Joqi rose slowly, keeping his head slightly lowered. He could see the large *szswn* clearly from this posture.

"Why did you come to our solar system," the leader asked.

"Exalted Leader, I came to study the massive brown dwarf planet," Joqi answered, as Cssyza instructed. Apparently the *szswns* classified the massive object as a planet.

The leader and the smaller *szswn* reared up slightly at the sight of Joqi shuffling his feet and gesturing with his arms to mimic the *szswn* language dance. All was quiet for several seconds, and then the leader assumed its previous dominating posture.

"Why do you wish to study the large planet," the leader asked.

"To complete our understanding of the nature of matter," Joqi replied

"That would be useful to us all," the leader said coldly.

The smaller *szswn* reached over and touched the large leader on a hind leg. The two conversed too quietly for Joqi to understand them.

"How did you get here," the leader asked bluntly.

Uh oh, Cssyza provided no guidance on how to answer this. Joqi decided to tell the truth, but not the whole story.

"In my advanced spaceship," he said, trying his best to avoid sounding condescending. "Such is the nature of our technology."

The small *szswn* on the platform started shuffling its legs nervously and Cssyza did likewise. The large leader remained calm, staring intently at Joqi.

"There is much we need to know about you and your ship," the leader said. "Humbled Cssyza will provide instructions for your journey here."

The communications link was unceremoniously terminated. In spite of the leader's controlled posture, Joqi sensed that it was very worried about what his arrival might mean for the future of its species.

Joqi turned to address Cssyza, who was still nervously shuffling its legs.

"What have you conveyed to your leaders," he asked, in as conciliatory a tone as he could convey in the *szswn* language.

"All that I have learned about you and your ship," Cssyza replied, calming down somewhat.

"I expected as much," Joqi said. But the short exchange with the arrogant leader aggravated him nonetheless. "Did you explain the self-aware nature of my spaceship?"

"Yes, and it caused great concern among our leaders and our scientists."

"What did your leader mean by calling you humbled Cssyza?"

Cssyza looked around the command center, its four eyes seeming to drink in every detail. Then it focused all eyes on Joqi.

"I no longer command," Cssyza finally said. No other explanation was offered; none was needed.

Joqi gritted his teeth, not liking any part of the leader's attitude or decisions. It was time to stand tall.

"Convey to your leaders that my spaceship will self-destruct before allowing any *szswn* to board it. Any vessels in close proximity will also be destroyed."

• • •

Dawn estimated the flight to the *szswns'* planet while pushing the damaged ship would take about thirty Zilan weeks. They still maintained Zilan time aboard the *Horizon Quest.* They could make it to the planet a lot faster if uncoupled from the *szswn* spaceship. Joqi made it clear to Cssyza they could push the damaged ship into a trajectory where it would reach the home world safely at a later time. Cssyza could join him in the *Horizon Quest,* and they could then accelerate quickly to get the *szswn* home. Cssyza understood, but still refused to leave its ship.

"I am responsible for this," Cssyza said, sweeping a fore-leg in an arc pointing at all in the command center.

Joqi recognized the gesture meant the entire space-ship. He understood its reluctance to leave its ship; he would have a hard time abandoning the *Horizon Quest* in a similar situation.

"Okay, Commander," he said, trying to lighten the mood Cssyza was retreating into. They were getting to know each other very well and had reached a basic level of trust of each other.

Joqi recognized a change in Cssyza after the communication with its leaders, but he couldn't quite figure out what it was. It was like Cssyza had accepted the situation as something that was inevitable, something that was orchestrated by an authority much higher than it was.

But even as their mutual trust solidified, Cssyza still insisted their continuing dialog be conducted via communication channels. As before, Joqi didn't push for in-person meetings. He was satisfied to stay in his plasma filled command pod for most of the journey to the *szswn's* home world.

He did follow Dawn's advice and meditated frequently. During those meditations, he isolated himself as much as possible from thoughts about existence in the smart plasma environment.

After a few weeks, Joqi decided to isolate himself physically from the smart plasma for short periods of time. He needed to prepare for direct interface with the *szswn* representatives and leaders. Cssyza said he would likely need to meet with the leaders on the planet's surface. The leaders had yet to share with Cssyza how they planned to interface with the human and his unique spaceship.

Joqi's first attempts to stay out of the command pod made it very clear that he was bound in intricate ways to the plasma; it was now an integral part of his existence. With no overriding reason for being out of the plasma, it was all he could do to stay out for an hour or two. It helped to engage Dawn in discussions about unsolved theoretical physics issues regarding undetectable matter and energy in the universe, which had long intrigued him. The discussions and insights were nowhere near as crisp and understandable as when discussed while he was immersed in the plasma.

• • •

Joqi rode an exoskeleton robot up the side of the *szswn* ship to the access airlock. It would take them another seven weeks to reach the *szswn's* home world, and Cssyza had asked for a meeting with him. It was about time; his patience was wearing thin waiting to learn what the *szswn* leaders had in mind for their arrival.

"Welcome Joqi," Cssyza said. It turned its back on Joqi. "Look at the results of your kind care in our first meeting."

There were string-like scars where the metal beam had cut into the *szswn's* back.

Cssyza turned to face him again. "I am fully recovered from the wound."

"I am glad," Joqi said.

He didn't know what a smiling *szswn* would look like, but he sensed Cssyza was feeling good and glad to see him. He sensed something else as well, an aura of contentment perhaps, as it looked at him.

"My leaders have a plan," Cssyza said. "I hope you will agree with it."

Cssyza explained how the *szswns* would interact when the two ships approached their home world. Several ships would intercept and escort the two connected ships into orbit. Once in orbit, they wanted Joqi to transfer to the damaged survey ship and stay in the command center with Cssyza. The human ship was to disconnect from the damaged scout ship and move far enough away to enable another ship to attach alongside the damaged ship. Joqi and Cssyza would then transfer to a *szswn* shuttle for transit to the planet's surface to meet the leaders.

*Dawn, the plan is okay with me in general,* Joqi conveyed. *Do you see any problem with it, other than it lacks details?*

*We need to work out orbital plans with the* szswns, Dawn replied. *And I am very concerned for your safety while on their planet.*

*I'll insist on limiting my time on the surface.*

"I assume we are being monitored," Joqi said to Cssyza.

"No, this is a private meeting between you and me," Cssyza replied.

Joqi believed the *szswn*. It was time to introduce Dawn, his "intelligent spaceship".

"Actually, it is a meeting among the three of us," Joqi stated. "My ship is always monitoring my activities and looking out for my wellbeing."

"Hello Cssyza," Dawn said via the wall mounted translator.

Cssyza stepped back, shuffling its feet slightly. It calmed down and stood quietly for several seconds before responding. It then interacted with Dawn, discussing details of the rescue activity. This interaction convinced Cssyza the ship was indeed self-aware and had its own personality.

"I understand," Cssyza finally said. "You two are close. My leaders would not understand. And neither would I, if not in closeness with you."

"Tell your leaders I agree with the plan in general," Joqi said. "Tell them I must be returned unharmed to my ship within two days of landing on your planet's surface. And I caution against any ship making a close approach to my ship."

Cssyza agreed to convey the message. It had a better chance than Joqi of doing so in a nonthreatening manner while getting the message across.

Cssyza indicated its superiors wanted much more information regarding the capabilities of his spaceship.

"I know you will not reveal much more about your ship," Cssyza said. "I have told my superiors its hull is made of an exotic material like none known to us. It has an advanced propulsion system, considering how easily it accelerated the combined mass of our two ships. Our scientists think it can jump through space-time, and this is how you came to our system. It has powerful weaponry, which I observed when it destroyed the incoming asteroids near the large planet. And the extensions of your ship, the robots, are amazing. Is there anything else I can offer them?"

"Give me time to interface with my ship," he said. "Then I will provide an answer." He was impressed by Cssyza's observations, but didn't correct the misunderstanding about the *Horizon Quest's* ability to jump through space-time. Let them believe that.

*I see what you are considering,* Dawn conveyed. *They will surely see the significance of it.*

"Tell them my ship can deflect or destroy asteroids as massive as the ship is," Joqi said, after a few minutes of silence.

"I understand," Cssyza said. "I will communicate this." After a pause, it then asked, "How do you communicate with your ship?"

Joqi smiled—the *szswn* had noticed there was no visible communication between him and the ship.

"We have a private channel." He offered no explanation and Cssyza didn't press for one.

He wondered just how far Cssyza would go in answering questions now that they had shared "closeness".

"May I share personal information and then ask you a related question," he said.

"Yes," Cssyza replied.

Joqi explained the procreation cycle for humans, and by Cssyza's lack of reaction, he sensed the *szswn* already knew about the human process. Then he popped his question.

"How does the *szswn* reproduction cycle work?"

Cssyza gave a short answer. The *szswns* had no separate genders like humans. Only one *szswn* was involved in their reproduction cycle, their "regen" cycle, from start to finish.

Remembering how he sensed contentment in Cssyza when he first arrived for the meeting, Joqi had an epiphany of sorts. Cssyza was pregnant; it had started a regen cycle.

"Are you undergoing regen," he asked.

Cssyza tensed up for a moment, and then relaxed. "Yes, I initiated regen after my ship was damaged."

Joqi sensed he was getting the truth, but not all of it. But Cssyza refused to provide more information about the *szswn* regen cycle.

Cssyza had remained cordial, if that was the right word for it, throughout their meeting. It again expressed great gratitude for the rescue by Joqi and his ship.

This brought the meeting to an end. To his surprise, Cssyza requested they meet in person weekly until arrival at the home world. This was good for several reasons, one of which he hoped the *szswn* never became aware of. He needed to practice functioning outside the smart plasma command pod.

# CHAPTER 12

Four *szswn* spaceships intercepted the *Horizon Quest* and its attached ship a week out from the home planet. They stayed their distance and tracked along with the *Quest* as it entered orbit around the planet. Apparently the captains of the ships were aware of Joqi's ship destroying several asteroids almost simultaneously.

Cssyza advised Joqi to stay in his ship until word was passed to detach the *Horizon Quest* from the damaged ship. This would be done at the appropriate orbital time to facilitate having a shuttle pick Cssyza and Joqi up, and then enter a short glide path to a spaceport on the surface.

When he received word from Cssyza to proceed, Joqi climbed into an exoskeleton robot and transferred to join the *szswn*. He instructed the robot to leave and join the other robots. The robots were detaching from the damaged ship and heading back to the *Horizon Quest*, which was moving slowly away. Joqi wore a spacesuit that contained backup oxygen and other supplies necessary to last a week on the surface. Of course, it would be a foul existence after a couple of days in the suit.

Once the *Horizon Quest* and the robots were clear of the damaged ship, one of the four *szswn* ships approached and docked with Cssyza's ship at the airlock chamber. Four *szswns* joined Cssyza and Joqi in the ship's control center. Each carried what looked like some type of weapon; they were taking no chances with Joqi.

The lead guard said, "Come." It then motioned for Cssyza to follow as it turned and headed toward the airlock chamber. Two of the other guards took up positions behind Joqi, and the third stayed behind in the command center.

Joqi and Cssyza were escorted unceremoniously through the airlock into the larger ship. No one greeted them. They were marched to another level in the ship where they were told to enter what looked like a shuttlecraft. Joqi hesitated for a moment until Cssyza motioned for him to follow. Four more guards were already in the craft, and motioned for them to strap into seats well back from the cockpit area.

*Dawn, can we communicate?*

*Yes, Joaquin, we can as long as your communicator works. The other alien ships have taken up positions around our ship, each about five kilometers away. All is well here. Be ever alert and cautious during your visit.*

No response was necessary. Dawn knew how he was feeling.

It wasn't until the shuttlecraft was launched into space that Joqi really began feeling withdrawal symptoms. He yearned for the comfort of his command pod!

• • •

It was a long trip from the spaceport to the council meeting building. Joqi regretted his decision to make landfall wearing only a spacesuit. The gravity became intolerable by the time he boarded the transport that waited for him at the spaceport. An exoskeleton robot would have helped tremendously.

The transport vehicle had a clear material covering the top half, and in the center of the compartment was a large, flat padded bench. Joqi felt like lying down on the bench, but resisted the urge. He needed to look as strong as possible in an environment that felt more oppressive as time wore on. It was obvious the vehicle was modified to show him off as it traveled through cavernous streets. The driver, and what Joqi surmised were guards, rode out of sight in the lower half of the vehicle. It was just as well; they became agitated when close to him.

His suit sensors showed the air was very acrid and it had an oxygen level about three-fourths what he needed to survive. It would be unwise to remove his suit helmet; he couldn't survive very long without auxiliary oxygen and the filters he wore in his nostrils.

*Szswns* lined the streets and more looked down from balconies, many pointing and gawking at Joqi. He stared right back, amazed at the sight of thousands of *szswns* along the way. Word apparently traveled fast among the general population. He had to turn his translator off to stop the loud din created by the multitude of *szswns* raising their voices. He could still hear them, but more as noise than as shrill words.

The structures along the streets had no visible windows, although many small balconies protruded outward. He looked straight up expecting to see the sky, but all he could see was a strip of bluish gray haze above the tops of the structures.

Something looked odd among those gathered along the way; all were of similar size and color. Were their young ones kept hidden? How could you tell a mature young adult from an old one?

Many more questions came to mind and Joqi wished Cssyza was beside him to answer them. He didn't know what to make of his friend being placed in a lower compartment at the rear of the vehicle. The last words from Cssyza at the spaceport cautioned Joqi to show great deference to the *szswn* leader, who, if angered, could react viciously.

The crowd noise hushed as the transport vehicle stopped in front of an imposing, deep violet colored building in the middle of a large open area. The guards motioned for Joqi to leave the vehicle, and then nudged him toward a long ramp that sloped upward to an imposing terrace jutting out from the front of the building. Guards stood beside intricately carved columns equally spaced along the terrace.

Joqi stopped at the foot of the polished rock ramp. A closer look revealed thin horizontal slits cut into the ramp about every half meter. Was this some kind of stairway?

His question was answered when one of his guards climbed quickly up the incline and onto the terrace above. He was shoved from behind, and fell forward to lay prone on the ramp. He started climbing as best he could on all fours. He had crawled no more than a couple of meters when two guards scurried up beside him. They grabbed him roughly under each arm and carried him to the terrace.

The two guards deposited him at the top of the stairs, and then pushed him toward a huge gaping opening from which a putrid smell emanated. It took a few moments for his eyes to adjust at the entryway. He could see guards positioned along a circular wall that appeared to extend completely around the huge chamber. He could barely make out an elevated structure directly ahead in the back half of the chamber. There were no visible monitoring devices, even though Cssyza told him the session would be transmitted live to the general population.

One of the guards stepped close from behind and pushed him on into the chamber. Joqi stumbled to a halt a few steps into the imposing structure. Remembering Cssyza's caution, he kept his head slightly bowed and eyes downcast as he moved slowly closer to the elevated platform, which was now bathed in light projected from above.

He sensed high anxiety among those present in the chamber, much more so than that detected earlier in his escorts from the spaceport. No, it wasn't anxiety. It was raw fear being covered by outward bravado. They were afraid of him—or of what forces were at play in getting him to their planet.

He had good peripheral vision and kept a wary eye on the guards along the walls as he moved cautiously to the middle of the room. Suddenly he heard a shrill squeal, causing him to stop. Was it a command, a warning, or a welcome? He had forgotten to turn his translator back on!

He reached for the translator control at his waist and in his periphery vision detected a flash of metal. A guard near the platform pointed what looked like a weapon at him. Joqi instinctively crouched and crossed his hands in front of his face as the weapon fired.

Time slowed for Joqi. What looked like a laser or ion beam was projecting out toward him from the guard's weapon. In the flash, Joqi saw the largest *szswn* he could have ever imagined stand up high on its eight appendages on the elevated platform, all its visual sensors glaring at him. Death was surely on him now!

A sphere of shimmering energy suddenly enveloped Joqi as the beam closed in. The sphere glared brightly as particles impinged on its surface and were immediately diffused and reflected around the room.

It was all over in an instant. Joqi was amazed to see all those in the room lying quivering where they had stood, including the huge *szswn* on the platform.

He turned and walked on shaky legs toward the chamber entrance. He was dazed and confused. Where had the protective shield come from? Could his EM field have activated and protected him? He tried to focus his thoughts, grasping for an explanation for what had just happened.

As he walked out of the chamber, several guards jumped on him before he could react. They pinned him down and held his arms so he couldn't reach his utility belt. One of the guards forcefully removed his suit helmet, scraping the side of Joqi's face and head in the process. The pain was intense, but he smelled a strange chemical and crumpled into deep darkness.

• • •

Cold...shivering...wet...burning—pain in all extremities. Joqi cautiously cracked opened crusted eyelids and was rewarded with severe burning pain. But the brief glimpse revealed he was in a metal cage partially submerged in churning liquid. Caustic liquid!

He licked his lips and tasted salty, gritty wetness that burned his tongue. He tried to salivate and spit to relieve the pain, but could not. Pain in other sensitive areas of his body was becoming unbearable. He took quick breaths through his nose trying to get enough oxygen into his lungs. Dizziness and nausea added to his discomfort.

In his quick look he saw a topside cage door that had some sort of lock on it. He was imprisoned and there was nothing he could do about it. He was in the surf of one of the planet's large oceans!

He shuddered as he remembered what Cssyza said about the high, rapidly changing tides on the planet. He had the feeling the tide would be coming in soon.

The *szswns* had stripped off his clothes and taken all his equipment. Fortunately, they left the filters positioned deep within his nostrils, or he would have already succumbed to the caustic air laced with bitter, salty mist from the dark surging sea.

Something slithered across his legs and, without thinking, he opened his eyes again. Through searing pain, he saw black, shiny creatures snaking through dark, breaking waves, and in the distance a burnt-orange sun dipping toward the horizon. He clamped his eyes shut, suffering through the intense eye pain. Right now any means of death would be welcome to end this nightmare, the quicker the better.

*Oh, Granpeda, I've done it now.*

A dull throbbing ache of despair started deep within; his survival while exposed in this environment would be short-lived and extremely painful. The harsh seawater was literally chafing his skin off and would continue until his soft body tissue was dissolved. It was no consolation to know he would likely pass out and drown before that process ran its course.

> *Imagine a man trapped in a cage*
> *sitting in the edge of the breaking waves*
> *caustic seawater eating his flesh*
> *dark creatures waiting for what is left.*

The ditty came from nowhere and repeated in his mind. He laughed hysterically, or was he just imagining he did. The line between reality and dream state was blurred as he sank to the bottom of a deep abyss of despair.

He began praying, dwelling on every word in the Zilan Prayer of Deliverance. It was customary to offer this prayer for someone who had just died, to ease that person's transition to the spirit world. It was his fervent hope that it would speed him along that path now. He had said the prayer three times when another thought intruded.

*Meditate, my Joqi.*

Startled, he gasped for air, and searing pain forced a hoarse scream from his burning throat.

A vision of his grandpapa formed in his mind, much like what happened when he meditated in the smart plasma aboard the *Horizon Quest.*

*Come, join me grandson.*

*Granpeda, if only I could.*

*You can, my Joqi. In your mind you can, you must to survive! Now, concentrate and dream of better things.*

His grandpapa was clearer now, extending a hand to encourage him to come along down a path to a grassy field near a clear, cool, flowing spring river. Ecina was sitting on the bank of the river on a carpet of green grass, smiling and waving. Two small children played by the water; a boy and a girl, and they looked like twins—he had fathered twins.

Joqi took his grandpapa's hand and rose to follow. Even if this was a dream, he welcomed it. All pain and worry dissipated as he embraced Ecina, and then turned to hug the children he was seeing for the first time. He loosened his hug and the twins ran to splash around in the shallows. He took Ecina by the hand and they went to join the rambunctious pair.

· · ·

Consciousness came slowly, up through a deep well of pain. When the pain became unbearable, Joqi retreated, dreaming again. But these were bad dreams, not of grandpapa, Ecina, and their children, but of dark things, hungry things, pursuing him at every turn.

The cage banged and clanged as something cut open the door on top. He passed out when rough appendages slid under each arm and pulled him forcefully from the cage.

Raw, inflamed flesh protested and rubbed off as he slid back and forth on the black, sandpaper surface of whatever was carrying him.

He passed out again as he was placed in a compartment that vibrated with raw energy.

• • •

He felt cold, colder than ice and in a place as dark as the farthest reaches of space.

*I will look after you.*

Joqi regained semi-consciousness, only to experience searing pain in every conceivable part of his anatomy. He could feel small creatures eating away at his flesh. He visualized hordes of small black bugs chasing him as he receded into unconsciousness.

# CHAPTER 13

*Joaquin! Joaquin!* A strong female voice echoed in his ear.

He swam upstream in the familiar, cool waters of the Avili, against a stronger current than he remembered ever encountering. Nevertheless, it was very refreshing to slice through the cold water with strong arm strokes. The aches and pains he felt earlier melted away and he yelled with joy.

He swam tirelessly against the current until he heard a low rumbling sound coming from behind. The sound increased steadily in volume, so he stopped swimming and looked downstream. Chill bumps rose all over his torso, and it wasn't due to the cold spring water. The river ended about 200 meters downstream!

No, the river continued. Mist rose over the jagged edge of a large waterfall, sending water tumbling into a gaping canyon. He couldn't see this, but he knew it was there. He turned and swam as fast as he could, but soon realized he was losing the battle. He changed his strategy, swimming at an angle to intercept the shore before spilling over the waterfall.

He was tiring and knew he wasn't going to make it to shore. A thin thread of reason touched his thoughts. He grasped mentally at the thread, pulling himself up out of the river just as he reached the waterfall's edge. He settled into a dimly illuminated place that felt velvety soft, where caressing undulations relaxed his mind and body.

· · ·

*Joaquin!* Dawn had never dared invade this far into Joqi's mind. It exposed his inner self to her and she felt like an interloper. But she was desperate, having tried all other possible avenues to revive him. The smart plasma was taking care of his physical wounds and had induced a deep meditation, a very deep coma. She searched for signs of activity and a way to stimulate him to revive and begin healing his psychic wounds.

*Joaquin, please awaken—I need you, our people need you!*

Her focused, emotional plea penetrated deeply and sharply, and Joqi stirred for the first time in several weeks.

Given hope, Dawn clasped the kernel of waking thoughts tightly and guided them toward that private meditation state where he locked out all awareness of being immersed in the smart plasma. But it was indeed the plasma that shielded him while he was in that most private of all places.

• • •

Joqi sat on the grassy bank of the Avili overlooking the deep pool below some rapids, his favorite place to meditate. He focused on the pleasant rippling sounds coming from the rapids just upstream. It was a very serene place, but it wasn't relieving his internal tension as it always had in the past.

He heard leaves rustling just down the bank. He tried to shut that sound out and focus on the relaxing sounds of the river flowing over rocks in the shallow rapids. But it was no use. The rustling sound grew closer and he knew someone was coming.

With a sigh, he rose from his grassy seat and looked downstream. His agitation at the interruption dissipated when he saw his grandpapa approaching. The prophet's gait was strong and he looked years younger than Joqi remembered. He was smiling as he approached, and Joqi felt infused with strength and love as the two hugged.

His grandpapa sat down in a meditative posture and Joqi followed suit. But his grandpapa had something else in mind rather than meditation.

"My Joqi, what are you doing here?"

Joqi frowned. What was he doing here? He felt a deep tension like none he had felt before, and he was here trying to relieve that tension.

"I am trying to figure that out, Grandpapa."

"The mind can play tricks on you," his grandpapa said. "To protect itself, it can deflect all sensory input about things external."

His grandpapa reached over and touched Joqi on the arm, the customary touch of respect and taking of peace gesture of the Zilans.

Joqi felt severe pain suddenly coursing throughout his body. He fell over on his side and curled into a fetal position.

"Sometimes the mind does not know when to stop protecting itself," his grandpapa said. "It keeps reviving painful memories to keep the mind introverted and protected."

Joqi felt his grandpapa's warm hands cupping his face. The severe pain eased and in a few minutes was gone. He sat up, the aftershock of the pain making him shake. That too subsided, and he heard again the rippling waters of the rapids. He turned to thank his grandpapa, but he was gone.

Joqi felt the presence of another. *Dawn?*

*Yes Joaquin, I am here.*

There was tenseness, a note of concern in Dawn's communication that he had never sensed before. The Avili centered environment dissipated in a swirl of fog. Joqi felt the forceful cushioning of the smart plasma, which was protecting him from what he surmised was high acceleration of the *Horizon Quest.*

*Is everything okay?*

*I should be asking you that,* Dawn replied tactfully.

Memory of his ordeal on the *szswns'* planet came rushing back in. He felt Dawn's thoughts embrace him like never before, concerned and protective, lifting him the rest of the way out of his virtual meditative state.

*I'm okay,* he conveyed, and he sensed her retreat slightly. *I remember what happened on the planet, and bits and pieces of being transported somewhere after that. Perhaps you should fill me in on what happened.*

*I will share my memories of events with you,* she replied.

He was immediately aware of what had transpired.

•  •  •

The leader and its guards in the meeting chamber were only stunned by the deflected ion beam from the guard's weapon. Once the leader revived, he ordered Joqi's sacrifice to the ocean creatures, as was the *szswn* custom for their dead. The leader ordered this done quietly and quickly so as not to alert Joqi's ship, giving *szswn* forces time to prepare to overcome the ship by force.

Dawn became aware that something was amiss when she tried unsuccessfully to contact Joqi via his communicator and by direct mind link. When the communicator went offline suddenly, she organized several robots for a search and rescue mission to the surface. She knew Joqi walked out of the meeting chamber, but from there his location was a mystery. She used high resolution imagery and monitored communications channels, attempting to find where Joqi was being held. She surmised correctly that he was a prisoner of the *szswns*.

Joqi's rescue by Cssyza surprised everyone. No effort was made by the *szswns* to thwart the rescue; Cssyza was the only *szswn* to enter the regen process in a very long time on the planet. The leader directed that all forces take a wait and see posture because Cssyza was approaching the final regen phase.

Dawn stopped short of launching the search and rescue mission when she intercepted communications regarding Cssyza's ongoing rescue efforts. Cssyza commandeered a space shuttle and communicated to Dawn that it was bringing Joqi to the *Horizon Quest*. Cssyza informed Dawn of Joqi's dire, possibly fatal, condition. Dawn had robots configure a temporary docking structure for the alien shuttlecraft.

Two robots boarded the shuttle once it docked with the *Quest*, and transported Joqi directly to the smart plasma command pod for immediate immersion. Dawn expressed deep appreciation to Cssyza for its rescue efforts and invited it to come aboard. Cssyza was quite content to do so, and brought along several containers of supplies it would need to survive. The shuttlecraft was then set adrift.

Dawn tried to link with Joqi, but could not. She decided the best approach was to let the smart plasma tend to his needs. She made sure Cssyza was safely settled in a small storeroom that was cleared and modified as the *szswn* brought Joqi from the surface. In a short dialog with Cssyza, Dawn learned it could safely withstand a lot more acceleration force than a human could.

That was all Dawn needed to know in the short term. She accelerated the *Horizon Quest* quickly away from the nearby *szswn* ships, setting a course that would intercept the nearby dying star. The ships stopped chasing after the *Quest* in three days; they were unable keep up.

Dawn chose the trajectory toward the local star because it offered several options they could consider for the next leg of their journey. The option she favored was to enter a partial orbit of the star, and then exit that orbit in a trajectory pointing out to the region of the brown dwarf. They had enough fuel to get there reasonably fast, but very little more. She hoped Joqi would awaken long before reaching the star and provide guidance on where they should go next.

Dawn had turned her full attention to Joqi, agonizing over his condition and her inability to protect him while he was on the planet. She reached out to him, but his deep coma prevented any contact.

• • •

Six weeks after leaving the vicinity of the *szsuns'* planet, Joqi felt strong enough mentally to engage Cssyza in conversation. He discovered a video projector was already in place in the *szsun's* compartment. Dawn told him Cssyza had made the journey so far in a semi-dormant state, but was now fully alert.

"Greetings, Cssyza," Joqi said. Only audio was projected into the compartment, although Joqi could see into the room. "May we converse?"

"Yes," Cssyza replied. "I have much to share with you."

Cssyza was shuffling its feet and nervously snapping its mandibles together. Joqi projected his simulacrum image into the compartment in the hope it would calm Cssyza. The *szsun* backed away from Joqi's 3-D image, and assumed its normal communications stance, rear end lowered to the floor and front end held higher by extended front legs.

"I apologize for the dire circumstances imposed on you by my kind," Cssyza said, in as sincere an expression as Joqi had seen from any *szswn*.

"You were not responsible," Joqi replied. "You saved me, and I thank you!"

"Where do we start," it asked. "You must have many questions and I have much I need to share with you."

"What I would like first," Joqi said, "is to understand why your leaders let you rescue me. They could have stopped you at any time before you boarded this ship."

"Because I am undergoing the regen process of my species," Cssyza replied. "No *szswn* has done this in over 200 years on our planet."

Cssyza paused, clearly struggling with what to say next, and Joqi waited patiently.

"You affected me from the moment you first shed your spacesuit aboard my damaged ship."

"You affected me also," Joqi replied. What he didn't say was how being close to Cssyza had surfaced raw fear first felt in his dreams before leaving the Zilan solar system.

"Not in the same way you affected me," Cssyza said. "Your closeness caused my regen cycle to start."

What Cssyza described next was beyond anything Joqi could have imagined. The *szswns* had maintained a symbiotic relationship with a sea mammal species, the *oscyspods*, as far back as any could remember. To initiate the *szswn* procreation cycle, a close bond was initiated with an individual of this sea mammal species. At some point this caused internal fertilization to occur, which started what they called a "regen", or regeneration process.

A multitude of embryos resulted inside the *szswn* adult, and when the embryos matured, a fight to the finish occurred among the newborn within the host adult. The final battles occurred around the nine "brain" modules of the parent. The nine strongest and smartest survived, and each turned to eat their hard won booty, one of the nine brain modules. Once they consumed the brains, absorbing most of the information content in the process, they ate through the host's body shell and exited.

The absorption of information by the newborns consuming and digesting the brain modules was almost unbelievable to Joqi. But he could believe it considering what he had observed in advanced studies when artificial intelligence driven machines gained knowledge by decomposing complex information storage structures.

The freed newborns had insatiable appetites to support their rapid growth. The *oscyspod* species provided their infirm and dead as food for the rapidly growing newborns in exchange for the remainder of the host *szswn's* body. The carcass was critical to the mammals; they needed the enzymes and other proteins, plus the concentrated calcium in the body, to sustain their own procreation cycle.

The *oscyspod* species had two genders, roughly equivalent to male and female in most mammal species. When ingested, the *szswn* enzymes induced chemical changes in the female mammal's reproductive organs, making her fertile and receptive to impregnation by the male of their species. The concentrated calcium in the carcass gave new-born *oscyspods* strong bone and cartilage structures. One carcass could support several female mammals through their birthing process.

The problem was the deteriorating condition of the *szswns'* planet, which led to decimation of the *oscyspods* as the ocean coastal regions turned more caustic. Volcanic activity had increased significantly in the past 2,000 years. And when they spewed volcanic ash into the atmosphere, acid rain fell for long periods, even after the volcanoes settled down waiting to spew forth again. This made standing water and rivers turn acidic, and it took longer and longer for the water to return to normal. The oceans fared better, except in coastal regions where the *oscyspods* normally ranged. The coastal regions ultimately received all the acidic land runoff waters which killed much of the aquatic life the *oscyspods* depended on for sustenance.

To address this problem, the *szswns* prepared and maintained a large inland body of water, a huge lake, where the chemical balance was constantly adjusted to support the *oscyspods'* needs. In time, this proved unsustainable, and the *szswns* next built several enclosed facilities containing the proper water environment for the mammals and supporting aquatic life.

The *oscyspods* were in essence subjugated to *szswn* control, for the express purpose of supporting the *szswn* procreation cycle. This worked well for the *szswns*, or at least for the select few that were privileged to participate in the regen process. It didn't work in favor of the *oscyspods*, which were reduced to breeding stock enslaved by the *szswns*.

Things got decidedly worse when some in the *szswn* society demanded fair treatment in selecting who got to regen. Adjustments in the selection process were made, but didn't satisfy the masses very long. The bottom line was that very few *szswns* at any level in society were going through the regen process. A revolt occurred, with many of the *oscyspod* holding facilities overrun by the rebels. This further decimated the mammal population and greatly diminished the *szswns'* hopes for long term survival of their species.

Once control was reestablished by a new ruling clique, the decision was made to launch select *szswns* and the remaining *oscyspod* breeding stock in generation ships to habitable planets in other solar systems.

At this juncture in the interaction with Joqi, Cssyza became very quiet before proceeding hesitantly with the rest of the story. Of the possible habitable planets discovered, the ruling clique sent the generation ships to two planets situated close along the direct path to Earth. If the *oscyspods* didn't survive the journey and reproduce as needed, and if no suitable replacement for the mammals were found on the planets, the generation ships were to proceed on to the vicinity of Earth. Humans were considered prime replacements for the *oscyspods* required to support *szswn* procreation!

"You affected me," Cssyza said, "from the first time I was exposed to you undressed during my rescue, and in later encounters. That started and sustained my regen cycle."

Cssyza slumped to the floor and stopped communicating after this statement.

*Now I know what the dark danger was that Grandpapa was so concerned about,* Joqi conveyed to Dawn. *I know the meaning of my dream about newborn* szswns *eating me alive.*

After a thoughtful moment, he added, *I wouldn't be surprised to learn the leaders believed Cssyza wanted to rescue and store me to feed its young.*

*You are not going to participate in completing Cssyza's regen process,* Dawn stated emphatically.

*No, I'm not,* Joqi mused. *But our real problem is figuring out how to stop the advance of* szswns *toward the human occupied region of space.*

# CHAPTER 14

It took a full two days before Cssyza showed a willingness to resume conversing. It was again by remote communication; the *szswn* showed great reluctance to have Joqi physically present in its compartment.

"I have much to thank you for," Cssyza said.

"It is I who must thank you," Joqi replied. "You saved me!"

He didn't add what was obvious; Cssyza had signed its death warrant and likely the same for its offspring, by rescuing him and boarding the *Horizon Quest.*

"Do you have other questions," the *szswn* asked. "My time is growing short."

"What can we do for you in this final regen phase?"

"Record completion of my regen cycle and send the recording back to my fellow *szswns.*"

Cssyza said nothing about caring for its offspring. It probably didn't know what to say. Joqi had a kernel of an idea forming, but didn't want to say anything until he thought it through and coordinated with Dawn. He elected to turn the conversation in another direction.

"What were you looking for in your survey of the large planet orbiting the brown dwarf," Joqi asked. He had asked about this when pushing Cssyza's damaged ship away from the planet, but it had refused to answer then.

"My mission was to determine if the planet is suitable for *szswn* colonization," Cssyza replied.

"The surface gravity of the planet is about twice that on your home planet," Joqi replied, with astonishment. "The 100 percent increase in body weight at the surface would be intolerable, even for a *szswn*."

"My survey revealed the surface gravity is about 120 percent higher," Cssyza said, correcting Joqi. "That is beyond what I could survive if I stayed on the surface very long."

Staying on the surface was the key phrase. Cssyza went on to summarize a plan borne from desperation by the *szswns* stranded on their home planet. In the near term, the plan called for residing in generation ships orbiting the large planet, and using robotic equipment to mine the planet for materials to support the orbiting ships' needs.

In the long term, the *szswns* had two options for those orbiting the large planet to survive the expansion and collapse of their star. Being on the outer edge of their solar system, the generation ships could head toward the closer of the two solar systems they had already colonized. The second option was to excavate large chambers deep within the planet, seeking lower gravity and shielded protection from the expanding star. The planet and the nearby brown dwarf would likely be pushed out of the solar system. And if it survived, the planet would in effect become a spaceship for the *szswns*.

It all sounded pretty far out to Joqi, but then, his home solar system was expected to remain stable for another two billion years.

• • •

Joqi reinstated his routine of meditating in a private virtual place designed to shut out all thoughts having anything to do with the smart plasma. He had yet to convey to Dawn the plan that was forming in his mind about where to point the *Horizon Quest* next. He still wanted to think about its implications, for he would have to leave the ship again. He would have to decide soon, for they were fast approaching the bright star.

He started meditating, but ended up daydreaming about Cssyza's regen cycle. Images formed and assimilated into a dream-like vision of numerous black insect-like creatures devouring an unrecognizable mammal's body. He felt no fear from the black aliens this time, even when the hoard of small creatures flipped the body over to reveal his own face. Joqi smiled and withdrew from his private meditation; he had made his decisions about Cssyza and where to go next.

Dawn's thoughts were never very far away from his— she hovered close like a concerned caretaker. This was okay with Joqi; Dawn and dreaming about his grandpapa had pulled him out of his deep coma. The experience bonded him and Dawn closer than ever before.

*How long will it take us to return to the* szswns' *planet?*

Dawn had sensed earlier he might want to do this, but with it now openly expressed, she was a little stunned and very concerned.

*Do you think I'll be well enough by the time we return to make another trip to the surface?* He could tell she was more than a little disturbed now.

*My actions now will dictate how humans will be viewed by the* szswns *in the future,* he added. *Cut and run gives one impression. Stepping boldly into the throat of our enemy sends another.*

*Only if you survive,* Dawn finally conveyed. *I am concerned about your health and your longevity if we take this course of action.*

*Prophet Sepeda, my grandfather, told me to follow my intuition when logic failed to address an issue adequately. My intuition strongly suggests I confront the leaders. They likely believe I am dead and already consumed by the offspring of Cssyza. My return will show a human's strength and courage.*

*But perhaps not a human's wisdom,* Dawn had to add.

This stopped their discussion for several minutes. Joqi wasn't upset with Dawn. She was just trying to protect him.

Dawn broke the silence. *I reluctantly agree, Joaquin. Based on your progress so far, you should recover enough by the time we orbit the szswns' world to leave the command pod for a short period.*

*That is what we'll do,* Joqi replied. *Calculate the necessary orbit around the star to loop us back to the planet.*

*As you command, Joaquin.*

• • •

Joqi sat in a straight-back chair facing Cssyza. Both intended to make this a short visit; he was still healing and the *szswn* was about to give birth, the start of its final regen phase. But they wanted to meet in person one last time. The *Horizon Quest* had looped around the bright star and was heading back to the home planet.

"Is this compartment large enough for your nine off-spring," Joqi asked, to start their conversation. They had relocated Cssyza to a larger compartment after modifications were made. Robots had installed access ports through which they would provide food and water to the newborns. The robots had also installed plumbing to maintain a more suitable atmosphere for the offspring, and to remove waste material. Dawn started recording activities in the compartment after Cssyza moved there.

"Yes, it is more than adequate," Cssyza replied. "Remember, at first they will act irrationally. Hunger will drive their actions as they grow rapidly."

Joqi was very mindful of this and had previously assured Cssyza the only direct interaction with the newborns would be by robots.

"The high protein meat product produced by our fab-ricators should keep them growing," Joqi said. "Did you find the taste of our latest sample to your liking?"

"Yes," Cssyza said with great appreciation. They had worked together to develop the artificial meat. "It is the closest thing to *oscyspod* meat that I can imagine."

He and Cssyza had already discussed how to handle the newborns once back at the home planet. They would have grown to over half Cssyza's size by the time the *Horizon Quest* reached the planet. Joqi still had to determine how to transport the newborns to the planet's surface. A lot depended on the *szswn* leader's reaction to the "regen" video he planned to transmit to those on the planet.

"Why are you taking steps to ensure survival of my species," Cssyza asked abruptly. "A *szswn* would take steps to eliminate a possible future threat, not encourage growth of that threat."

Good question. How could he explain his intuitions role in his decision?

"I would rather have a strong ally than face a desperate enemy."

"You are wise, for a human," Cssyza said, emitting the closest thing to a chuckle Joqi had heard from it.

Joqi smiled and said, "As you are for a *szswn*."

Joqi had a curious question come to mind. "How do *szswns* tell each other apart? How can we distinguish each of the nine newborns from the others?"

"Each *szswn* is distinguished from birth by emitted odor and the markings along the edge between our top and bottom halves. Additional markings are added throughout the life of a *szswn* to recognize major accomplishments and service to our society. "

Cssyza paused, and then added, "You should concentrate on the markings. The difference between emitted odors is very subtle and sometimes even confusing among groups of *szswns*."

Joqi looked closely at the front edge of Cssyza's body. He could just make out fine markings that had gone unnoticed by him and Dawn. He was glad he didn't have to distinguish between several *szswns* by smell; the emitted odors made him nauseous.

"I have wondered about the extent of the memories you pass to your newborns," Joqi said. "If the newborns receive memories of the close *oscyspod* or mammal relationship that stimulated the regen process, what keeps them from also starting regen when recalling those memories?"

"The significance of the regen process for our species survival is passed along," Cssyza said. "But the close personal feelings affecting the parent causing the regen process to start are not passed along. Otherwise, the newborns could relive the experience and initiate their regen process too early in life. Regen normally occurs late in life."

This meant that all *szswns* on their home world were now late in life. This was a stunning revelation and Joqi didn't know what to say.

"One last thing, then you must go," Cssyza said. "We have exceptional memories and we live long lives. Many memories are from the distant past, passed down generation after generation through the regen process. We are creating an exceptional memory for my newborns to share far into the future."

Cssyza then stepped closer and raised its two front legs, pointing the two claws toward Joqi. He rose from his chair and placed his hands on the claws. It was as much a touch of respect and a taking of peace as any Zilan gesture could be. Joqi was glad the *szswn* had learned early on that he didn't like emitted odors. After a brief moment, Cssyza pulled its claws back and Joqi turned to leave, knowing it was the last time he would see his alien friend in person.

# CHAPTER 15

Joqi watched Cssyza's regen process run its course from the comfort and safety of his command pod. He felt no fear this time, just compassion for his alien friend who was giving its life to start a new generation.

The scene playing out in Cssyza's compartment was strikingly similar to what Joqi visualized in dreams while still in the Zilan solar system. It was unsettling in that respect; how had his subconscious mind known what a *szswn* looked like. And more disturbing was the question of how he had visualized the regen process when there were no known records of this on Zilia or in the data Dawn had pilfered from Earth's records. There were forces at play that he would likely never understand.

He shook this thinking off and focused back on what was happening in the large compartment. The newborns were moving around just under Cssyza's tough skin, looking for a way out of the carcass. Based on what Cssyza had said, it died quickly as war raged inside, each newborn vying for dominance near one of the nine brains. The dominant newborns then quickly consumed the nine brains and began looking for a way out. One finally chewed through the skin and exited. The other eight followed quickly. Joqi wondered just how many of Cssyza's memories now resided in the young ones.

On cue, a robot pushed a slab of fabricated meat through one of the three feeding portals. Joqi watched anxiously as the nine small *szswns* swarmed to the meat. If they didn't eat, all leverage was lost in the plan to present the newborns to the home world leaders.

The newborns tore into the meat with a vengeance, quickly reducing it to a greasy spot on the feeding tray. Joqi was relieved that the newborns found the fabricated meat to their liking. Still, he was concerned about what this could mean for future encounters between humans and *szswns*. They had to halt advance of the *szswns* toward human occupied worlds!

Two additional meat trays were pushed through the other feeding ports, and the infants swarmed there, quickly devouring two more slabs. It was curious that the newborns were not fighting each other for the meat. It might be a different story if the food were in short supply.

*Our meat fabricator can keep up with the demand,* Dawn conveyed. *A backup fabricator is ready to come online if needed, and the additional machines you asked for are nearing completion. I estimate we have enough raw ingredients to feed the newborns for two months. Then we will need to replenish our resources.*

He smiled; she was indeed closely monitoring his thoughts. They would be in orbit well before running out of food for the newborns.

Joqi had an insightful thought while watching the newborns eat. The newborns absorbed information when consuming the host *szswn's* brains. The first food they ate outside the host's body was *oscyspod* meat. This must further ingrain in the newborns' memories the key role *oscyspods* played in completing the regen process!

*Send the video of Cssyza's regen process up to this point to the* szswns' *planet,* Joqi conveyed. *Include a snippet of a healthy me overseeing the process. Send it repeatedly until we get a response.*

• • •

The *szswns* did not respond right away to Cssyza's regen process video, and Joqi's attention turned to the dilemma he and Dawn would face after he met with the leaders. Where should they go? Was there even a remote chance of their ever getting back to Zilia? Should they make their peace with the *szswns* as best they could and stay in their solar system?

He pondered these questions, and more, as he transitioned to his private, deep meditation place. But to his surprise, it wasn't his special place on the bank of the Avili. He stood on top of an atoll, looking across verdant farm fields stretching to the horizon in one direction, and bounded in the other by a meandering river, probably the Avili.

The fields were familiar, laid out in patterns similar to those in cooperative farms on Zilia. In the nearest fields he could see the green-tipped yellow flowers of the tuchera plant. The bright flowers meant the tuchera plants would soon start producing long green vegetable pods that were a staple in the Zilan diet. He relaxed; it felt like home.

He heard someone whistling far away, and then coming closer. He saw a man striding along a path leading up the small hill to where he stood. He smiled and waved at his grandpapa, who waved back and kept climbing at a strong pace. Joqi walked down to meet the prophet, who smiled and embraced him.

"This is a beautiful place to meditate, is it not," his grandpapa said as they walked to the top.

Joqi had to agree as he looked at the panoramic view of the farms and tree lined river, all under a cloud free blue sky. It was peaceful and relaxing, and they sat down side by side in the middle of the atoll on comfortable matted grass.

"Why are you here, my Joqi," his grandpapa asked.

Joqi frowned. He had heard that question before.

"Granpeda, I am seeking answers to our dilemma—how to return to this place." He swept his right arm to encompass the scene all around them.

"At first glance, the universe is an inhospitable, distant place," the prophet said. "But if you look at it in just the right way, you can overcome even the seemingly impossible challenges."

The only movement in the broad vista before them was a large bird lifting gracefully from the top of a tree near the river. It flew in circles, higher and higher, until its majestic flight brought it high overhead.

His grandpapa laid a hand on his shoulder and looked up at the bird soaring in the aqua blue sky. "Until now you have used about half your brain's capacity for cognitive reasoning. Granted that is much more than most of our kind uses. Imagine what you could do if you applied the total capability you have."

His grandpapa's comment sounded a lot like what his father had said before he started fulltime immersion in the smart plasma pod.

"But I have no control over how much of my mind is used."

"How much higher do you think it can fly," his grandpapa asked, pointing up at the soaring bird.

Joqi recognized the bird was an adult red-beaked hawk. "It primarily hunts small game and rodents. If it goes much higher, it cannot see its prey."

"True," his grandpapa replied. "Your answer is biased by your knowledge about the hawk. It has eyesight that is ten times as good as yours, yet it only uses that advanced capability to search for rodents."

His grandpapa paused and watched the hawk circle in flight high above them.

"I ask again, how much higher can it fly?"

"Much higher," Joqi answered, beginning to understand. "But it probably never will."

"How much higher can you fly, my Joqi, if you shed your knowledge biases?"

• • •

The *szswn* reply to the repeating video of Cssyza's regen experience was cautiously positive. The *szswn* making the response was of average size compared to others seen in the background. There was no sign of the large, combative leader Joqi had previously encountered.

The *szswn* introduced itself as Azlor, the newly elected leader. Azlor then turned and introduced the *szswn* positioned slightly to the rear. Lotsu was Azlor's deputy and second in command.

"You honor us by making it possible for Cssyza to complete regen," Azlor said. "We are amazed and most appreciative of your ability to feed and take care of the newborns. You have our deepest apology for how you were treated when last honoring us with your presence. We humbly ask for your forgiveness."

Azlor continued with an invitation for Joqi's ship to enter a close orbit of the *szswns'* world. The leader recommended a plan for transferring the newborns to the planet's surface, at Joqi's convenience. The plan involved a shuttlecraft docking with the *Horizon Quest* to pick up the youngsters. Azlor was very polite and humble when requesting Joqi transfer the capability to produce food for the newborns. The leader requested that Joqi provide Cssyza's remains so they could honor the *szswn* by offering its carcass to sea creatures, as was the *szswn* custom.

The leader recognized that Cssyza and Joqi had developed a close relationship, and it expressed the desire to work closer with him as well. The leader ended the message by inviting Joqi to once again meet with the *szswn* leadership, this time with guaranteed safety.

*You are healing well,* Dawn conveyed after watching the video message. *But I ask that you stay aboard our ship.*

Joqi didn't respond. She could sense his decision.

• • •

Dawn guided the *Horizon Quest* into orbit around the *szswns'* world, as discussed with their leader. The orbit was close enough to support shuttlecraft transportation to and from the surface, and high enough to avoid interfering with the many satellites orbiting the planet. No ships came near the *Quest.* Joqi had made it clear to the leader that any attempts to damage or board his spaceship, or to injure him again, would incur the full force of retaliation by his ship.

The young *szswns* were over half the size of Cssyza and were talking fluently when the shuttlecraft arrived to take them to the surface. The nine newborns, two meat fabricators, and ingredients to make more meat were transferred smoothly to the shuttlecraft. The fabricators were programmed by Dawn for automatic operation based on the eating habits of the newborns. Their appetite was still strong, but reduced significantly from what it was right after they exited Cssyza's carcass. Operating instructions for the fabricators were also provided. They had preserved Cssyza's carcass in cold storage, and it was transferred respectfully to the shuttle.

Joqi decided to wait a few days before having the *szswns* transport him to the surface for meetings with their leader and council members. Azlor agreed; it would give time for the fuss about the newborns to subside, and for the *szswns* to honor Cssyza's carcass.

And plenty of fuss there was, as Joqi and Dawn monitored activities from orbit. Joqi couldn't imagine how overjoyed those on his home world would be upon seeing a newborn child for the first time in over two centuries.

Joqi had stayed in the command pod, for the most part, while they traveled back to the *szswns'* planet. He was still undergoing repair by swarming nanobots and other agents in the smart plasma. He tried to spend several hours out of the plasma each week in preparation for another visit to the planet's surface. He never made it to more than five or six hours before giving in to the overwhelming need to get back into the plasma.

*I feel less and less comfortable while out of the smart plasma pod,* Joqi thought.

*I have observed as much,* Dawn replied. *The private meditation sessions are not as effective as before. Have you considered taking part of the plasma with you when out of the pod?*

Why hadn't he thought of that? Joqi liked the idea, and he knew by Dawn bringing it up that it was possible.

He proceeded to test the suggestion immediately. Lying calmly immersed in the pod, he visualized a thin coating of smart plasma covering him from the neck down. He knew the plasma could do it; every time he entered the pod the plasma greeted him by smoothly crawling up his body. But how would it react when he walked away from the pod?

Joqi commanded the pod hatch to open. The plasma stayed in the pod, helped by the light spin gravity in the command pod compartment. He stood up and waited until the plasma retreated from his body—which it did, except for a thin layer of shimmering, pink tinged plasma coating him from the neck down.

He climbed out of the pod and walked a few paces away, surprised that no plasma footprints were left behind. He looked at his arms and hands; the plasma looked like a thin, translucent skin spread evenly over his anatomy. He didn't feel the immediate urge to return to the pod as he always had before.

Satisfied with the test, he climbed back into the command pod. He relaxed and again his thoughts turned to the issue of what they should do after their liaison with the *szswns*.

His meditations during the early phase of the trip around the local star had focused primarily on getting well, physically and mentally. But in recent weeks he had focused more and more on the challenges they would face after leaving orbit around the *szswns'* planet. This focus was stimulated in part by questions his grandpapa had raised.

His grandpapa! Had he really talked to him? Joqi became less sure of this the longer he thought about it. It was more likely his subconscious mind was playing tricks on him, tricks surfaced while in deep meditation while immersed in the smart plasma. But it was difficult to believe that his subconscious mind was at play when thinking about how his grandpapa lifted him out of his unbearable misery in the cage overflowing with caustic seawater.

Regardless, the questions raised in his recent meditations were certainly stimulating him to look at issues and his environment differently. And the paramount question was—what were the knowledge biases limiting his assessment of his environment? And not just the elements that he could sense directly applying all the capabilities embodied in the *Horizon Quest*. What about the other 95 percent of what the universe was made of that he couldn't directly sense?

These ruminations brought to mind a noted Zilan mathematician and philosopher he had met and studied under. At a young age, LaSorepe Kilerah had postulated how undetectable energy and matter in the universe could interact with the small amounts of observable energy and matter. LaSorepe was the grandson of the revered High Priest Pilone Kilerah, who became Carlos Sepeda's close friend as he walked the path to become Prophet Sepeda.

The equations were beautiful to view, artistry on a level few ever achieved. However, very few people could fully understand the complex mathematics that incorporated octonion algebra to define extra dimensions in space-time.

Joqi attended several lectures by Professor Kilerah regarding the structure of the universe some fifty years after the mathematician first presented his theory. The professor and several others had made concerted efforts throughout the intervening fifty years to prove elements of his theory. But to no avail.

What if Professor Kilerah and others had accepted that his theory was basically correct? Joqi had come to believe it was when attending the professor's lectures. He wondered now what the professor and various other teams could have achieved during that fifty years if they had focused on developing extensions to the theory instead of trying everything imaginable to prove the basic theory. But they were locked into the paradigm that had existed for centuries, where physical proofs of grand theories were required for them to stand the test of time.

He began consciously challenging boundary conditions that limited his understanding of Professor Kilerah's theory and other theories defining the space-time continuum. He felt sure that somewhere in extensions of those theories lay the answer about how to get back to Zilia. And the answer must be found while they were in the *szswns'* solar system. Otherwise, it would be a very long, slow journey back to Zilia, with no assurance of survival for him, Dawn, or the *Horizon Quest.*

# CHAPTER 16

Joqi looked out the shuttlecraft's porthole and shuddered at the memory of his last trip to the world's surface. What destiny awaited him on this second trip? He couldn't clear the destiny thought out of his mind. Was it his intuition driving his actions now, or the guidance of some greater power?

The shuttlecraft flight to the surface was uneventful, other than his unsettled thoughts. He recalled the effect his grandpapa had on the Zilan population as he quietly espoused his religious beliefs through exemplary actions, not words. For the first time in several years, Joqi said a quiet prayer asking for guidance during his pending meeting with the *szswn* leaders.

The shuttlecraft landed at the same spaceport as before, on the outskirts of the capitol city. This time he was greeted by two delegates from the ruling council, who bowed low before escorting him to his transportation. His suit sensors detected a foul gas surrounding the delegates, which dissipated quickly. He detected a puzzling sense of awe in their posture and welcoming statements. Perhaps it was unusual for anyone to ever escape from their sacrificial cage.

By the time they walked the short distance to a transport vehicle, Joqi regretted again his decision to come to the surface without riding in an exoskeleton robot. The 40 percent increase in gravity over that of his home planet made it very difficult to walk smoothly. But he needed to show strength during this visit without relying on mechanical support.

The transport vehicle was the same one that was used on his first trip, with the upper half enclosed by a transparent semicircle canopy. The two delegates climbed into the top half of the vehicle with Joqi, and took up positions at the back of the compartment. The round bench had been moved to the front half of the compartment, and now sported a chair in its center that was hand carved with various swirls and other intricate features.

The artwork on the chair was beautiful and surely had meaning to the *szswns*. Joqi had to smile. Placement of the regal chair and the presence of the greeting committee sent the message he was viewed quite differently this time around. He climbed up on the platform trying to hide how the exertion strained him. He sat in the ornate chair, which was appropriately sized for him while wearing a spacesuit. He was thankful for its support as the transport accelerated smoothly away from the spaceport.

Thousands of *szswns* again lined the streets along the route to the council meeting, but this time they were eerily quiet. Many pressed close for a better view, slowing the vehicle and finally bringing it to a stop. Joqi felt uneasy, but remained calm, as did the two delegates in the rear of the compartment.

They were trying to see him, he finally realized. But all they were seeing was something clad in a bulky space-suit. On impulse, he removed his suit helmet and placed it beside the chair. The crowd stopped pressing forward and remained quiet. Joqi thought back to his final interaction with Cssyza, and raised both hands like he had when saying goodbye to the *szswn*.

Those nearest to the transport raised both front legs, and the others behind started doing likewise. He heard a high pitched hum start among those close to the vehicle, and increase in volume as those farther away joined in. The humming increased in volume until the chair he was sitting in began vibrating slightly. He looked over his shoulder and saw the two delegates approaching the round bench with their two front legs raised, pointing toward him. They stopped at the edge of the bench, continuing to hold their front legs out toward Joqi.

*Thank you, Cssyza,* he thought. *You were one wise* szswn!

His two nostril filters did a good job of minimizing the acrid smell of the air, but the low level of oxygen was apparent immediately. Deep breaths through his nose filters helped, but he finally had to plug a small oxygen line into one nostril, tapping the suit's supply.

There was a commotion up ahead as several guards pushed through the crowd, clearing a path for the transport. The transport began moving ahead slowly, with guards on each side and in front to keep the crowd of citizens from pressing in too close. Joqi held his arms up periodically throughout the journey to the council building. This elicited the same response from those in the large crowd as it had the first time.

Upon arriving at the large council building, one of the delegates climbed out of the vehicle and motioned for Joqi to follow. They walked to the bottom of the sloped stairs leading up to the council chamber, and Joqi had an uneasy moment when he was asked to stop. To his surprise, the other delegate scurried over carrying the regal chair and set it down facing the sloped stairs. At the delegate's invitation, Joqi sat in the chair and placed his helmet in his lap.

Three guards hurried over and picked up the chair with Joqi in it, one on each side and one behind. They scurried up the sloped stairs, keeping Joqi and his chair level with the street, and set him down on the terrace facing the large entryway.

Joqi rose and nodded to the guards, and then walked confidently through the large entryway into the huge, round council chamber. The two delegates followed a few paces to the rear. He held his head high with eyes looking forward, not a deferential posture at all this time. He had turned his translator on at the spaceport and he remained in constant contact with Dawn via a communicator. She was concerned about him leaving his helmet off but understood his reason for doing so.

Joqi stopped a few steps into the chamber to let his eyes adjust to the dim light. It was startling to see all *szswns* in the room in a submissive posture, the front of their bodies lowered to the floor and the back of their bodies elevated. There were three *szswns* positioned on each side of a slightly elevated platform toward the back of the chamber. There were two average sized *szswns* on the elevated platform, and both were also in the submissive posture. No weapons were visible anywhere in the chamber. This time he noticed what could be video camera pods mounted at various points around the ceiling.

He walked slowly toward the elevated platform, the pull of the high gravity taking a toll on his posture. He stopped about three meters from the platform base, then stepped back a pace when the platform started lowering. He laid his helmet on the floor so he could use both arms when communicating. In a few seconds the platform stopped level to the floor, with the two *szswns'* posture still showing deference to Joqi, which seemed more than a little odd to him.

"Chosen One, may we address you?"

He wasn't sure which of the two had spoken. Why address him as the Chosen One? Why ask if they could address him?

"Yes, please face me," he replied evenly, surprised at this turn of events.

The two smoothly raised their frontends and lowered their back ends, which was their normal posture for communicating. The one on the left backed away one body length, deferring to the one in front.

The front *szswn*, evidently their new leader, looked intently at Joqi with its four eyestalks while its legs quivered nervously.

"What do you mean, Chosen One," Joqi asked, in a more conciliatory tone.

"For generations our kind...awaited arrival of the Chosen One."

The *szswn's* vocal glands then uttered rapid clicks and squeals that came across as noise through Joqi's translator. The *szswn* behind the one speaking let out a strong series of clicks that, as best the translator could tell, meant "Enough!"

"I am Azlor," the front *szswn* said, its vocal glands settling down. "I speak for our species. The others here are members of our ruling council." It pointed with its two front legs at the three *szswns* positioned on each side of the platform.

Azlor then puffed air through its vocal glands, air that bellowed out to engulf Joqi. It was more rancid than any foul human gas he had ever smelled.

*Caution*, Dawn conveyed. *Remember—that is the way* szswns *greet one another with honor.*

"I am honored," Joqi said, realizing the foul gas detected around the two delegates at the spaceport had meant the same thing.

This seemed to calm the leader. "None of our species has regened on this planet in over 200 cycles—none until now."

This made less sense now than it had when Cssyza explained it. 200 cycles, or 200 years on this planet, was a lot longer than any Zilan had lived. The leader was implying that all those lining the streets along the ride to the council building were over 200 years old!

*This is truly remarkable,* Dawn conveyed. *I was unsure that Cssyza was telling the truth about this.*

*It explains why no small ones have been observed,* Joqi replied.

"How does this relate to my arrival," Joqi asked the leader.

"You were the stimulus," Azlor replied. "You caused our Honored Cssyza to start regen. You provided the food necessary to complete the regen cycle. My deputy, Lotsu, will explain."

Azlor moved backward and Lotsu moved forward. Joqi endured another blast of foul air, without flinching this time.

"Chosen One honors our species," Lotsu said. "I store and convey through offspring our species history. So honored we can now fulfill that destiny."

Joqi patiently listened to the clipped language presentation made by Lotsu. Apparently the species had a philosophy based religious culture. For thousands of years they had believed they would someday face a crisis in ability to propagate their species. A venerable leader had prophesized that a Chosen One would someday provide a solution to enable their species to propagate and fulfill their rightful place in spreading their culture among the stars.

The *szswns* had always believed the Chosen One would be a *szswn*. To have it be an alien from some distant place was almost incomprehensible at first. They were astounded when Joqi survived his ordeal as their sacrificial offering to the sea. Their astonishment and respect over his relationship and support for Cssyza and its nine offspring made them believe he was the Chosen One.

*Dawn, why didn't you tell me this before I came back here?*

*If I had told you, would you have come back?*

"Chosen One, why did you allow us to capture you on your first visit," Azlor asked. The leader had moved forward beside its deputy. "You have great power. You demonstrated such in the first meeting. How could we subdue you so easily when you left our Great Hall?"

Joqi straightened up as tall as he could in the higher gravity. He extended his arms, palms outward, toward Lotsu and Azlor.

He spoke loud and added flourishes with his arms, feet and translator panel to fully communicate with the leaders. "I allowed you to take me so that what has happened would happen.

"I returned to show the strength of my species," Joqi continued. "You should not want us as your enemy, nor do we want you as ours." He hoped the translator accurately conveyed the essence of what he said.

The two leaders and the others around the chamber wall started shuffling nervously. He had seen this reaction in Cssyza when it became unsure about something or felt threatened.

"We have great power as individuals and as augmented with our advanced technology," Joqi added. "I suffered so you would see what we could withstand and how strong our resolve is to survive!

"We want to avoid conflict with your race. Both of our species can grow and prosper in our own regions of space."

"Chosen One, you honor us with this understanding," said Azlor, who stopped shuffling its feet. "For over 400 years we have received and analyzed signals emitted by your civilization. The rapid advancement of your technology and your aggressive nature disturbed us greatly."

"That was on Earth," Joqi replied. "I am from the planet Zilia."

He asked that the chair be brought in so he could sit while they conversed. The strong gravity was wearing on him and he was willing to give up some flourishes in speaking with limited feet movements.

Azlor motioned to a *szswn* near the entrance, and it brought the chair in quickly. Joqi thanked the leader and sat down. It was time to get to know one another a lot better before the oppressive gravity wore him down completely.

# CHAPTER 17

Joqi felt a moral obligation to help the *szswns* regain their vision of surviving and thriving. However, he did have a problem with their plan to continue expansion in space toward human colonized worlds. His condition for providing help was the commitment by the ruling council that their species would colonize no additional worlds in the direction of human occupied worlds. He had no problem with their two current colony worlds prospering; he didn't like the idea they viewed humans as substitutes for the sea mammals.

The ruling council readily agreed. Joqi recognized that at some point in the future, hopefully several centuries later, interaction between *szswns* and humans was inevitable. His resolve to help the *szswns* strengthened when Azlor told him candidly that their colony worlds would soon face the same procreation problem that existed on their home world. And the end game was clear if nothing changed. Very few *oscyspods* survived the journey to the new world colonies; too few to sustain growth in their population.

After three hours of interaction that was grueling for Joqi in the high gravity on the surface, he told Azlor he must return to his ship. He set up and demonstrated a 3-D communications projector they could use to continue interaction. And he agreed to return to the surface for in-person meetings every few days. He advised that on the return visits he would ride in a robot exoskeleton to help maneuver around on the surface. Azlor and the council agreed with this approach for continued interaction, and once again thanked Joqi sincerely for his help with Cssyza's regen process, and for bravely returning to face the council.

In parting, Joqi said, "Intelligent life in the universe is very precious. I believe most species die out before ever achieving the plateau of self-aware, questing conscious-ness that humans and *szswns* have. I believe other species are out there that have achieved the level of awareness we have. They remain undetected by our search efforts. However, our two species must be prepared for the chal-lenges presented by future contact with such advanced species."

"I speak for humans of the planet Zilia," Joqi contin-ued. "On my return home, our government will inform those on other human worlds about your species. We will focus on forming an alliance among the human occupied worlds that will recognize the value of having you as allies. This will take well into the future to achieve."

"You are wise in our eyes, Chosen One," Azlor said. "We agree and look forward to facing that future with humans as allies."

The return trip to the spaceport was made in the same transport vehicle that carried Joqi to the council meeting. He found a box next to the elevated bench containing the spacesuit he wore to the first council meeting. The suit was damaged where the guards had ripped off the helmet on his first visit.

The translator and all other equipment he had carried to the surface were also in the box. He had to smile at finding his equipment; the *szswns* were making amends as best they could for what occurred on the first visit.

Apparently no announcement was made to the general population as to when he would travel back to board the shuttlecraft. The same two council delegates that met him at the spaceport accompanied him back there.

The delegates stayed close to the elevated bench and were eager to engage Joqi in conversation. Joqi learned that most *szswns* resided in compact underground dwellings. The above ground buildings were only a small part of the extended habitats.

He could see that doors into the buildings along their route were about half as tall as he was. The delegates confirmed that hallways and rooms in the buildings also had low ceilings, but that common areas where residents convened to socialize had ceilings that were several floors high. He hoped he would never need to go inside one of the dwellings; just thinking about it raised claustrophobic feelings.

"What do *szswns* eat," Joqi asked the delegates. No farms were visible from the *Horizon Quest*, although they had observed many ships at sea that could be fishing vessels.

"We make *surlii* from raw minerals," the delegate on the right answered. "*Surlii* is our primary food. This is supplemented with creatures and plants harvested from the sea."

The delegate described *surlii* as a thick, porridge like soup, which was piped to feeding stations throughout the city. Citizens could access the feeding stations at will. The creatures and plants taken from the sea provided additional ingredients necessary to balance their diet, and were prepared in public kitchens throughout the city.

"Do you harvest and eat any *oscyspods*," Joqi asked?

"We have found no *oscyspods* in our oceans for a very long time," the second delegate said sadly. "We never consumed *oscyspods* unless it was part of the regen process. They were considered our equals thousands of years ago."

"What do humans eat," the first delegate asked.

Joqi described the wide variety of plant and animal products that humans consumed. He also described the many ways products were prepared to provide variety and stimulate the taste buds. The delegates seemed confused by the idea that humans varied their diet for pleasure.

"Do you get pleasure from eating," Joqi asked, guessing what was confusing the two delegates.

"Consuming food is necessary to survive," answered the first delegate. "That is its value."

"Now we understand why your food fabricators are much more complex than ours," the second delegate said.

"What do you do for entertainment," Joqi asked. He wanted to know more about the personal lives of the *szswns*. This seemed to puzzle the delegates, so he explained various activities humans engaged in for sport and enlightenment.

"We share experiences and generation history," the first delegate finally answered.

"We engage in philosophical discussions," the second delegate added. "We quest for better understanding of the *Everything*."

"By the *Everything*, do you mean all in the observable universe?"

"Yes, plus all you cannot see," the second delegate answered. "We strive to become one with the *All*."

*As I do through meditation,* Joqi thought.

"Do you have games you play in competition," he asked. He explained the Zilan game of crossball.

"Not as you describe," the first delegate answered. "We constantly play thought games, challenging each other to find better explanations for the *Everything*. Also, special design activities, such as complex communication systems, become team competitions for the best design."

"Sometimes when linked we sense vast reaches of matter and energy in the unobservable part of the *Everything*," the second delegate said. "This occurs when enough of us having similar philosophical ideas link and focus on the unobservable."

"How do individuals link and communicate when separated by great distance in the city," Joqi asked. There were no antennas visible anywhere along their travel route, and no utility lines of any kind were apparent to support communication. None of the *szswns* had carried portable communication units that he could see.

"Let us demonstrate," the second delegate said.

It began emitting the same high frequency hum the crowds had emitted on the trip into the city. The first delegate joined in, and then Joqi heard similar hums come from a few overhead balconies. Soon there were *szswns* on most of the balconies, adding to the concert of hums.

"We have established social links with the many," said the first delegate while it continued to hum. "Those close to us link with citizens farther away, expanding the network to all in the population that want to participate."

"Participate in what," Joqi asked.

"In our joy at sharing closeness with you," the second delegate said.

*Uh oh, I better opt out of this sharing business,* Joqi thought.

*You are probably only affecting the two delegates close to you,* Dawn conveyed.

Joqi was relieved to see they were approaching the spaceport. He had one other curious question for the delegates before disembarking to board the shuttlecraft.

"How many *szswns* reside on your home world?"

He was surprised at the answer—the population was less than five million, with most of them residing in the vicinity of the large city they had traveled through. Their global population had shrunk to a small fraction of what it was at the peak of their civilization. Having no one undergo regen in the past 200 years was only a symptom of the problem. Global environmental deterioration on the planet over the past several thousand years was the real culprit.

On the shuttle flight back to the *Horizon Quest*, Joqi mentally reviewed what was accomplished while he was on the surface. He had made sure the *szswns* knew how to operate the food fabricators and could provide the raw materials required to support the machines continued operation. He learned the *szswns* had a communications system comparable to the Zilan Hycoms system that enabled fast communication over stellar distances. News of what was occurring around the home world was shared in near real time with their colonized worlds. A short discussion with the *szswns* about this communication capability revealed it was not compatible with the Zilan system.

Joqi had agreed to keep his ship in orbit around the planet for several more weeks, but he expressed the desire to return soon to the brown dwarf for closer examination of it and the large orbiting planet. He wasn't sure why he chose this path. At least the decision would provide time to look at other options for leaving the solar system. He had a nagging question about the brown dwarf sub-star; how much matter was actually tied up in the massive dwarf's deep gravity well? A better estimate would provide a partial answer to where all the undetected matter was located in the universe, the so-called dark matter comprised of weakly interacting massive particles, among others.

In the discussion with council members, Joqi had subtly brought up the question of how they intended to address the regen issue since they no longer had any *oscyspod* mammals to initiate the process. And he wasn't about to stay around to work his charm on other *szswns* like he had with Cssyza.

The regen issue discussion caused quite a stir among the council members. It became obvious they had no plan, but considered it the most critical problem to solve if they were to survive. Joqi had some ideas, but elected to explore them more before discussing any specific solution. He asked several questions to support sifting through options, and discovered a *szswn* never dreamed. They were a very logical, pragmatic species that never even daydreamed. The connection between dreaming and fantasizing was strong in humans, and fantasizing and anticipating the sexual act often heightened arousal. He had concluded discussion of the regen process by requesting every bit of data available regarding the special *oscyspod* sea mammal species.

Even with the thin coating of smart plasma, Joqi was ready to collapse by the time he lay down in the command pod. It was a very draining but productive trip to the planet's surface.

• • •

*Hey Dad, wake up.*

*Dad?* Joqi heard the confusing query while in a light meditative state. It brought him to full attention in the smart plasma. Was this a joke by Dawn?

*No joke,* Dawn replied. *But I guess I am learning more of the human mannerisms.*

Joqi smiled in spite of the fact no one would see it.

*Okay, what does this dad reference mean?*

*You in effect fertilized Cssyza by your close proximity to it. And now you have done the same to the two delegates that accompanied you to and from the council meeting.*

Joqi sat upright to view the virtual control center display that Dawn opened. He reviewed the surface communications that she had intercepted. There was no doubt about it; the two delegates were celebrating starting their regen process.

But what about those exposed to him in the council chamber? There was no mention of any of those individuals in any communication. Come to think of it, they had remained farther away from him than the two delegates had during the trips to and from the spaceport.

*I'm not about to hang around jump starting the regen process for a long line of* szswns. *There must be a better alternative.*

The next thought came like a lightning bolt—the *szswns* were capable of fantasizing if they got a nudge. They just didn't realize it. He had provided the nudge Cssyza and the two delegates needed.

*I have an idea...*he started to convey.

*I see it,* Dawn interjected. *It should work.*

*Set up a communication link with Azlor and Lotsu.*

Minutes later Joqi's projected simulacrum stood facing the two leaders alone in the council chamber. The two stood a goodly distance away even though they knew his projected image was not real. They exchanged brief greetings, and then Joqi began explaining why he wanted to meet.

"In discussions with you and the other council members, I came to the conclusion those of your species do not dream or fantasize about events."

"That is correct," Lotsu said. "As you described dreams and fantasizing events, they do not occur in our species."

"Does a *szswn* have subconscious reasoning and automatic control functions in its nine brain modules?"

After he explained the functions he was asking about, Azlor and Lotsu affirmed that such functions were active in an adult's integrated mind modules.

"Then I believe an adult does fantasize about the regen process when near the appropriate stimulus, and this starts the process. The fantasizing occurs within the subconscious thought processes."

Both *szswns* began shuffling their feet, but remained quiet. So Joqi continued.

"The stage is set for this fantasizing when a newborn consumes *oscyspod* meat for the first time after leaving the host's body. Then much later, when an adult is ready for regen and encounters an appropriate mammal, the subconscious mind initiates the regen process."

He sensed that Lotsu was starting to accept the idea, but Azlor became agitated thinking about this possibility.

"This is a new and difficult process to accept, I know," Joqi said quietly. "I propose a simple test to see if this is indeed what happens. Let my ship project a virtual environment into a large surface facility that simulates the natural setting in which a *szswn* associates with an *oscyspod* to start the regen process. Then let a volunteer spend some time in the simulator relating to the sea mammal in something close to its natural environment"

This proposal caused both Azlor and Lotsu to retire to the far end of the chamber. Joqi waited patiently and avoided looking in their direction as they conversed in

private. After a few minutes, the two returned to their previous positions, and Lotsu addressed Joqi.

"You are the Chosen One. Therefore we give serious
consideration to your proposal. With some difficulty, we
accept your proposal, contingent on our council's approval.
We go seek that now."

They turned to leave, and then Azlor turned back to
face Joqi. "You should proceed with preparations for the
test. Lotsu presents very strong arguments for his causes."

• • •

Joqi and Dawn reviewed the *oscyspod* data, which were sub-
stantial. They needed the details to support programming
a virtual environment setting that realistically portrayed
the sea mammal in its natural environment.

Their dark gray bodies were long and sleek, with strong
flat tails that were half again as long as their body proper.
Their bodies had a fin sticking up in the middle. The fin
had a breathing tube up through its middle with an opening at the tip of the fin. The *oscyspods'* tails provided powerful motive force for the creatures when swimming and
when moving on land. Overall, the sea mammal's length
was about twice as long as Joqi was tall, or about four meters
long.

Joqi was astonished to learn that *oscyspods* had no eyes.
They had wide stripes down both sides and a roughly square
panel on their sloping foreheads. The stripes and panel
essentially provided Doppler radar scanning to enable the
mammals to "see" their surroundings. The square panel

also provided the means to communicate with others of their species and with the *szswns.*

An *oscyspod's* body was covered with fine bristle hair that pressed smoothly against its skin when swimming, and fuzzed out to increase how large it looked when threatened. Bacteria thrived in the hair to eat harmful microbes and pollutants to minimize skin infections. When exposed to the atmosphere, hair movement caused the mammal to look dark blue-gray with iridescent purple highlights.

In addition, an *oscyspod* had a large mouth centered in the blunt nose of its tapered head. The mouth slits crisscrossed, and when opened wide, they revealed a chamber filled with cilia, long hair-like filaments that strained small creatures from sea water for food. The outer edge of the mouth was ringed with sharp teeth; a diet of small creatures filtered from the sea water was insufficient to sustain an *oscyspod.* There were gill-like slits just behind the head, which served as exit ports for sea water taken in through the mouth.

An *oscyspod* also had leg-like appendages a little behind each of its gill slits. The two legs looked strong, with rotor joints where they connected with the body, giving them almost full circular movement. Each leg had another joint about halfway down the leg from the body, and appeared to function like an elbow. A stumpy, two-finger claw was at the end of each leg.

The legs supported movement on land, in concert with the tail. The mammal moved on land by pressing its front legs against or gripping the surface, then arching its back pulling the rear forward, then pushing against the surface with its tail while releasing its leg hold on the surface. This pushed the front half of the body forward. The mammal then repeated the hunching and pushing action to make its way across the surface. It could move surprisingly fast on land.

Once details about the *oscyspods* were assessed, Dawn programmed a virtual environment of a scene along a rough beach that had waves rolling in from an open sea. Joqi reviewed several videos of *oscyspods* frolicking in a frothy sea near shore, with several of the mammals splashing their way up onto the beach. He interacted with Dawn until the movements in the simulated environment were realistic.

The major challenge was to simulate what a *szswn* would feel if it touched a sea mammal's skin. Dawn programmed 3-D projectors used to establish the virtual environment so molecules of air would vibrate against an adult's claw if it touched the boundary representing the mammal's skin.

Another challenge was simulating how an *oscyspod* would respond to queries from a *szswn*. Joqi had several communications with Lotsu before they could pin down realistic *szswn* to *oscyspod* conversation scenarios.

Joqi also coordinated with Lotsu to have sand and rocks spread along one half of a large hall-like room to provide the appropriate feel to an adult walking across a beach. Sea water plumbing was installed, with hidden spray nozzles in the ceiling to simulate mist cast ashore by breaking waves. Scent projectors were added, and variable speed fans rounded out the physical aspects of the simulation. No *szswns* were allowed into the room once the sand, rocks and plumbing were in place. Then portable projectors were installed by Joqi's robots, and the whole scene was fine-tuned by him and Dawn to look and feel as real as possible. The projectors had video cameras to provide feedback to the ship. Joqi insisted that no *szswn* except the volunteer view what transpired in the room.

The day of the test had the ruling council in a nervous state, especially since they were not allowed to view what was going on. They had so many volunteers for the test that they had to select one randomly. One of Joqi's robots led the volunteer into the darkened simulation room blind-folded, then removed the blindfold and departed.

Joqi was proud of the end results in constructing the environment, even though the projected virtual scene was nowhere near as good as what he experienced immersed in the smart plasma. He watched closely as the volunteer walked cautiously farther into the virtual environment scene. Surely it knew the scene was a simulation, but Joqi was counting on the *szswn's* subconscious thoughts to assimilate enough from the sensory stimulus to initiate the regen process.

The adult *szswn* walked to the middle of the beach and reached out curiously to see if the flat rocks there were real. It seemed surprised to discover the rocks were indeed real. It climbed up on the first of three large flat rocks, and turned to look at the rolling waves flowing under an overcast dark sky. It raised the front part of its body, look-ing like a creature surveying its turf. Suddenly two *oscyspods* broke the surface just off the beach. They frolicked there for several minutes, capturing the attention of the adult.

After frolicking back and forth along the beach, one of the mammals headed for shore. The *szswn* reached out and communicated with the *oscyspod* as it rode a wave up onto the beach. The mammal raised its head as if sniffing the breeze, and then hunched and straightened its back in sequence to push itself to the rocks. It lay down at the foot of the rock the adult occupied, moving its flippers and making squealing noises. The *szswn* moved its legs nervously, and then reached down with one pincher leg to stroke the mammal's back. The *szswn* calmed down, then lay down on the rock, still stroking the mammal's back and communicating with it softly.

After several minutes, the *oscyspod* rose and hunched its way back to the water's edge. It splashed into the waves and swam to join its companion. Variations to the virtual environment sequence repeated for several hours, and then a small robot entered with a mask to cover the *szswn's* eye stalks. The robot led the volunteer out of the simulation room while the virtual environment continued to run.

After three sessions in the simulator over two days, the volunteer confirmed its regen process had started. Azlor, Lotsu, and the other members of the ruling council were in awe of what Joqi and his intelligent ship had accomplished.

# CHAPTER 18

**W**e have done all we can for now to counter the future threat of the szswns descending on Zilia, Earth, and Earth's colonies, Joqi thought.

*I agree,* Dawn conveyed. *This was the quest Prophet Sepeda sent us on. The* szswns *need warm blooded mammalian flesh to complete their reproductive cycle. They were focused on getting it eventually from habitable planets having ample populations of mammals—and eventually human occupied planets.*

What was their next step toward getting home? Joqi still had no idea. But he knew deep inside there was a path back and that he must find it. He was confident his grandpapa wouldn't send him on a dead end mission. But he had some unease; how could his grandpapa see what the future held? Or was he just making educated guesses?

There was an intermediate task that provided good reason to leave, as he had explained to the ruling council;

conducting a close assessment of the brown dwarf and its planet. He had promised to provide the results of that assessment to the *szswns*.

He couldn't explain the need he felt to survey the brown dwarf sub-star. Some of the feeling surely came from their entering the solar system at a point near the dwarf. Whatever or whomever opened the way from the Zilan solar system to this solar system, could just as easily have dropped them on the opposite side of the solar system from the brown dwarf. He had to trust his intuition which supported returning to the vicinity of the brown dwarf.

They had taken care of last minute details to support building and maintaining more virtual environment simulators that would induce the *szswn* regen process. It was time to leave.

Azlor, Lotsu, and the six council members had convened in the council building. Joqi projected his simulacrum into the imposing, circular chamber, which was well illuminated for his convenience.

"Greetings, Chosen One," Azlor said. All the *szswns* were in deferential postures in a semicircle, with Azlor in the center and Lotsu on his right.

Joqi was still uncomfortable at their calling him the Chosen One and showing deference to him. But there was nothing he could do about either.

"Greetings Azlor, Lotsu, and distinguished council members," Joqi said. "It is time for my ship and I to leave for the brown dwarf sub-star."

"We understood this day would come, but hoped it would be some time later," Azlor said. The council members were now in their normal posture, standing with their body level with the floor. Azlor and Lotsu were in their communication posture, with their frontends slightly elevated.

"We share memories and experiences widely among our kind," Lotsu said. "We will long remember the renewed hope you have given our civilization. Knowledge of the Chosen One and what he accomplished here will be remembered for all generations to come."

"Humans no longer need to worry about aggression from our kind," Azlor added, touching on a sensitive topic in earlier discussions with Joqi.

After the general goodbyes, the six council members departed, leaving Azlor and Lotsu to close out communication with Joqi.

"We plan to conduct a very thorough survey of the brown dwarf sub-star," Joqi said.

"We encourage you to take your time," Azlor replied. "The longer you stay in our planetary system, the more we are blessed."

Joqi had to smile at this response; the longer he stayed the more he could help if they encountered problems building more regen stimulating virtual environments.

"We will take our time and provide you our survey data."

He agreed to communicate periodically with the two leaders during the survey activities, and that completed their communication session.

• • •

Joqi deferred control of the *Horizon Quest* to Dawn and she turned the sleek spaceship outward from the planet. She deployed the ships huge solar sails to use the local star's radiation pressure to steadily accelerate the *Horizon Quest* outward. They needed to conserve their nuclear fuel, which was in short supply. There was no need to hide this secondary propulsion technique from the *szswns,* for they already used this technology. The acceleration created by the solar wind was low. However, it was continuous and would propel the *Horizon Quest* to a fairly high velocity toward the outer reaches of the solar system.

He could feel the smart plasma continuing the healing process. It was like an itch all over that scratching didn't relieve. His mind was crystal clear even though his body was still recovering. He kept searching for an elusive idea on what they should do next. He sensed that Dawn was also searching for a solution to their dilemma as she kept watch over the ship's systems.

Joqi reviewed again every bit of information Dawn had collected and catalogued about the local solar system. He looked closely out beyond the large outermost planet for the first time since they had rescued Cssyza. He was unable to find any indication of the transition point where they came into the solar system, except for a location Dawn had affixed to the data.

Asteroids were scarce in that region, but there was a thin belt of small asteroids beyond the outermost planet by a distance approximately the same as that between the outer planet and the brown dwarf. The fragments were probably the remains of a planet that never fully formed.

The large outer planet and the brown dwarf may have robbed the belt of most of its material, preventing formation of an additional planet. What was important to Joqi was they could mine the asteroids to replenish their raw resource needs, and possibly to manufacture more nuclear fuel for the *Horizon Quest*.

They would surely need more fuel. The *szswns* were no help when it came to providing nuclear fuel. They had experimented with nuclear devices in their distant past and decided such devices were too dangerous to their species and their home planet's environment. From what Joqi and Dawn had discerned, the *szswn* spaceships used some type of advanced ion plasma engine when exploring their solar system.

In any case, the prospects for using any fuel beyond surveying the brown dwarf looked dim, unless they could find another intersection point that would open a path back to Zilia. Without such a path they had only two options that he could think of. They could remain in the local system or point the *Horizon Quest* on a trajectory to intercept the closest human occupied planet in the distant future. He had no desire to go into extended hibernation in the smart plasma with the hope of being rescued by those on New Earth, the Earth colonized world that was twelve light-years closer than Zilia was.

He and Dawn had discussed time and again what occurred during the *Horizon Quest's* passage through the intersection point and transition to the *szswn* system. Joqi gained very little insight from these discussions to advance his understanding of the physics of a multidimensional universe, which he believed they resided in.

He needed more data to understand the relationship between ordinary observable matter and the unobservable things in the universe. The latter had surely played a role in getting them to this solar system. He had the nagging feeling again, like he had right after transition to this system, that this relationship was key to finding a way back to Zilia. But they couldn't even detect their exit point from the anomaly that deposited them in the outer reaches of the solar system several months earlier.

It seemed foolish to create a mood enhancing virtual environment now, but with no solution coming to mind, that is what Joqi did. Once again he imagined sitting on the bank of the Avili spring river on the co-op farm his parents managed on Zilia. The breeze gently rustled the leaves of the large shagba hardwood tree he sat under enjoying the shade from the relentless sun. He heard water rippling over rocks in the shallows just above the deep pool he faced, adding another familiar dimension to the environment.

Joqi noticed several bitternuts lying on the bank where they fell from the shagba tree. He picked one up that lay nearby and rolled it around in his palm, admiring the smooth, dark-brown shell. Little climber rodents loved the rich meaty seed inside, and stored as many as they could to help them survive the cold winters. In early times before modern farming techniques were developed, many Zilans survived tough times by storing and eating the bitternuts as well. But some had also died from eating the raw seeds.

Joqi liked the seeds when they were properly processed and roasted. He cracked open the shell with his thumbnails and popped out the moist, light-brown seed.

It looked good and smelled good, but from experience, he knew better than to pop it into his mouth. The bitternut seed had a high concentration of tannic acid in its brown surface. To leach out the toxic tannic acid, early Zilans learned to soak the nuts for several days in cool moving water, preferably flowing spring water.

Joqi smiled as he reminisced about roasting the nuts when camping as a young teenager. The first time, he and some friends had roasted the nuts without leaching out the tannic acid. Talk about stomach cramps and lower bowel pain!

Joqi tossed aside the enticing bitternut seed. Caution was certainly appropriate when trying things for the first time. You had to look much deeper than surface appearances to learn the true nature of things.

He looked at the river's surface, trying to see into its depths. The cold, clear water beckoned to him, but he resisted, still trying to peer under the surface to see what was hidden there. Even though the spring water was clear, the sunlight's angle and the reflections from the opposite shrub lined bank kept him from seeing below the surface. He knew the bottom of the river hosted a variety of life, from microscopic bugs to large fish and frogs and other critters. He just couldn't see any of them from his vantage point.

His grandpapa's words from long ago echoed in his thoughts. "Joqi, if you test the water you won't want to go in."

Joqi laughed as he stood up; in this case, he had gone in before. He ran and dove into the cold spring river, seeking the gravelly bottom and any aquatic creatures making it their home. He surfaced in the middle of the river and swam back to the bank. He sat again, but this time exposed to the warming rays of sunlight that began drying his clothes.

He assumed a meditating posture and the river and banks faded away as he focused elsewhere. He now knew where the answer to their dilemma lay.

• • •

"Sometimes we sense vast reaches of matter and energy in the unobservable part of the *Everything*," the *szswn* delegate had said. This comment was made when the two delegates escorted Joqi to the spaceport after his meeting with the ruling council. Joqi thought about this now, and about what Lotsu had said later about their scientists linking together to formulate theories regarding the unobservable matter and energy in the "Everything". If linked *szswn* scientists could "sense" the unobservable matter and energy in the universe, why couldn't he?

Joqi reached out mentally as he had done many times during the journey in the *Horizon Quest*, his thought sensitivity greatly enhanced by the smart plasma. He sensed systems and structures of the spaceship, now familiar as old friends. He briefly touched the core processing center that housed Dawn's private consciousness of self, and observed the vibrant processing ongoing there. He felt a stirring as she detected his presence. He reached farther, through the skin of the outer hull and on into the vast vacuum outside, which wasn't empty at all.

He detected specks of dust and molecules of helium and hydrogen, and more sparsely, some dense organic molecules. On average, there was a molecule or speck of observable matter in about every cubic meter of space in the region the *Horizon Quest* was passing through. But these molecules and specks were not what he was looking for.

He opened his mind farther, augmented by the smart plasma and the powerful sensor systems of the ship, to sense radiation in the local region around the spaceship. There was a flood of it, from full spectrum radiation from the local star to high energy particles from far-flung sources. He searched this radiation for any anomalies and found none. He began integrating everything detected into a comprehensive, multidimensional representation of space around the *Horizon Quest.*

On close examination of the integrated data, he detected a minute deflection of microwave radiation when integrated over long distances. There should be similar deflections of radiation in other wavelengths, but none were readily apparent, so he concentrated on the microwaves. But try as he might, he couldn't detect what was causing the deflections, the very low frequency modulation of the microwaves. He knew something was there, just as he knew there was something under the surface of the Avili spring river when he couldn't see past the surface reflections.

Like the ESP slug Alandi's team was investigating before he left Zilia, he was sensing the surrounding space with a capability that was hard to define. The integration of the *Horizon Quest's* sensory capabilities with his own, coupled with the smart plasma sharply focusing his mind, led to his sensing the environment surrounding the ship in a unique new way. It was as he imagined the linked scientists sensed the "Everything".

Joqi let his thoughts flow with the microwave radiation. He sensed something pulling on the microwaves, something in the darkness through which the radiation passed. He let all his senses free to embrace the darkness, filtering out ordinary matter and energy—everything directly observable.

At first there was nothing but a deep well of darkness, a dark firmament; nothing went in, nothing came out, or at least that was his first impression. He focused on an arbitrary spot in the darkness and looked closer and closer, and finally sensed massive dark particles. He couldn't see them; he sensed their presence through the miniscule disturbances they caused in the fabric of space-time. It was like some all-powerful entity had opened a keyhole for him into another realm.

He attempted to forge in even closer, trying to see between the particles. In doing so, he detected a slight movement of the particles away from his focal point. He was focusing enough energy to crack the keyhole open!

In his excitement he lost focus and just as suddenly was back observing radiation and ordinary particles in the area around the *Horizon Quest.*

*I need more processing power,* he thought. He remembered what his father and grandpapa had said about him using only half his brain's capability. How could he learn to use his brain's full capabilities?

*You have already done so,* Dawn conveyed. *Your new way of sensing the fabric of space-time reveals this.*

*But it isn't enough,* Joqi lamented.

• • •

Joqi continued to hone his newfound ability to sense unobservable features in the vacuum of space through which the *Horizon Quest* traveled on the way to the brown dwarf. He was unable initially to achieve any more than he had on his first try after leaving the *szswns'* home planet. But he remained optimistic and kept trying.

A rough image began taking shape in his mind of long rivers of dark matter spreading throughout space, sculpting in large part the shape of the observable universe. And he sensed a thin cloud of dark matter enshrouding the Milky Way Galaxy. He also felt the pressure of energy contained in the vacuum of space, and observed that it existed everywhere that he explored. This had to be the so-called quantum vacuum energy, the dark energy, which was causing the universe to continually expand.

*This experience is surreal,* he thought after another foray into the dark firmament. *It is like a dream that becomes clearer each time I enter the dream state of mind.*

*Or like a vision,* Dawn observed. She had monitored his thoughts during the most recent forays into the dark firmament. *Your grandfather, Prophet Sepeda, learned much from visions that helped guide his team and the Zilans through many difficult times. Accept what you sense. The knowledge will help us find our way back to Zilia.*

*I'll continue trying,* Joqi conveyed.

When not focused outward, Joqi focused inward, assessing the various theories that attempted to tie together all aspects of the universe in a unified theory. He was more a mechanobiologist than he was a physicist, but his mathematics background was strong. He researched the data Dawn had accumulated before their departure from the Zilan solar system. He looked at everything addressing dark matter and dark energy, those things in the universe that were not directly observable. With his recent observations, the theories made more sense to him now than they did before embarking on the mission.

He was able to reduce the number of potentially viable theories about the *Everything* to two. One was a theory pulled from the Earth archives pilfered by Dawn at the start of their mission. The theory, proposed in the mid twenty-first century on Earth, combined the Einstein general theory of relativity with the most accepted estimate of the structure and influence of dark energy and dark matter in the universe. This undetectable energy and matter were thought to make up most of the energy and matter in the universe. Joqi discovered questionable assumptions used to make the theory's equations balance when addressing gravity at the micro, or very small scale. However, the theory looked sound when addressing local structure at the macro, or large scale.

He found more promise in the theory proposed on Zilia by the mathematician LaSorepe Kilerah. Of particular interest was Professor Kilerah's theory about how undetectable matter, dark matter, influenced the formation and shape of galaxies through its gravitational pull on observable matter. If this was true, then observable matter exerted a pull of equal strength on dark matter as well. However, the greatly dispersed ordinary matter would have immeasurable small local pull on the concentrated filaments of dark matter. The professor had devoted the rest of his life trying to measure the attractive force between observable and unobservable matter to prove his theory.

*How much higher can you fly, my Joqi, if you shed your knowledge biases?*

His grandpapa's words echoed in his thoughts, and he smiled, remembering interacting with him on the high atoll overlooking far reaching farms. Yes, he now understood—if Kilerah's equations were correct as far as they went, he needed to build on them, not spend valuable time trying to verifying them.

# CHAPTER 19

Joqi reached up to scratch an itch on his scalp while contemplating professor Kilerah's equations. He felt bumps where it itched. He carefully explored the rest of his scalp using both hands. His head was covered with soft, bulbous bumps!

*I have a problem, Dawn. I think I'm having a reaction to the plasma.*

He activated the body scanner that was embedded in the walls of the command pod. The results came up quickly in a virtual 3-D display. His conscious mind rejected what he saw—all his head, except for his face, was covered by the bumps. The scan also showed strands forming a network directly interconnecting the bumps.

*The smart plasma is reacting to your demand for more cognitive ability,* Dawn conveyed. *The soft bumps are neuronal brain matter, added processing modules linked directly with your brain.*

He should have been horrified, but he was not. The plasma was doing what it was supposed to do—providing for his needs.

*I have sensed growth in my cognitive ability since I first detected dark elements in space around us. I didn't question where that growth came from. I thought it was from my using the full capability of my brain and mind.*

*Do you wish to stop the growth,* Dawn asked. *If it continues, it will likely become irreversible.*

Joqi paused to think about the consequences, but only for a few seconds. The scan showed his head no longer looked like that of a human. But he needed more brain power, more stochastic processing capability.

*No. If we are to find a way back to Zilia, I must continue on this path of discovery.*

Dawn did not respond. She would not weigh in either way on his decision.

Joqi felt completely healed. In fact, he felt better than he ever had, in spite of concerns regarding the bumps still growing on his scalp. He had no idea how far this brain extension process would go; he still needed more processing capability to "see" into the dark realm, the dark firmament, of the space-time continuum. He decided to stop scanning his body and to not worry about the growing bumps. He needed to focus on defining extensions to Kilerah's equations.

He "looked" many times into the dark firmament, grasping at understanding the tenuous interaction between ordinary matter and dark matter. These observations led to extensions to Kilerah's theory that explained the structure and interaction of the dark particles he detected. This in turn pointed to focal points in the observable universe where interaction between the observable and unobservable dimensions were concentrated. These focal points existed within massive observable objects, such as brown dwarf sub-stars, stars, and black holes. Was this why they were guided to enter this solar system near the brown dwarf?

Joqi's attention was pulled back into the *Horizon Quest* as they rapidly approached the brown dwarf sub-star. They planned to enter a survey orbit around the brown dwarf that was closer than the planet orbiting the dwarf. Dawn would then conduct a series of measurements to determine the brown dwarf's mass and composition, and to measure its tremendous gravity more accurately. They would also determine the orbiting planet's mass as accurately as possible, which would help in determining the brown dwarf's characteristics.

*The brown dwarf and its orbiting planet are a little odd,* Dawn observed. *Zilan astronomers determined long ago that brown dwarf's usually form in pairs.*

*I agree,* Joqi replied. *Perhaps the large outer planet in this solar system is a failed attempt to form another brown dwarf.*

Dawn remained silent for several seconds before responding. *If the mass of the brown dwarf and the large outer planet were combined, the resulting mass would be sufficient to start a fusion reaction in its core, forming a new star.*

*Yes, a possible future star to reset the life of this aging solar system,* Joqi conveyed.

This was an interesting line of speculation, but Joqi focused back on Kilerah's equations with his added extensions. His extensions brought to bear recent insights on the role gravity played in the interaction between observable and dark matter. He needed to know more about the dark particles.

He reached out again with all his senses, but now with sensitivity the module extensions to his brain amplified greatly. He sensed every facet of the spaceship, right out to the outer layer of atoms in the hull. He sensed the particles in the space closely surrounding the spaceship, and even the minute variations in the density of the particles. He continued reaching outward in the surrounding vacuum, enthralled by his expanded sensitivity. If this was a vision, it was the most realistic vision he could imagine!

Joqi sensed matter that heretofore had stayed hidden. The matter was comprised of massive particles which interacted weakly with neighboring particles, plus a variety of other dark particles that had no electric charge. He sensed the tremendous stored energy in the surrounding vacuum that had stayed hidden from human probing. The energy was overwhelming at first, and then became less so as his expanded senses and processing powers absorbed understanding of the dark energy and dark matter.

Weak forces and hidden matter thus revealed opened Joqi's enhanced comprehension to a level never achieved by the greatest human minds. He sensed gravity variations amplified by the dark energy throughout the vacuum of space. He could see the localized weak gravity fields combining on a large scale.

The dark matter gravity fields shaped the space-time continuum. The dark matter existed everywhere, even flowing through him as he thought about it, although it was concentrated more in areas of high ordinary matter content.

*What value is all this knowledge in our quest to return to Zilia?*

This introspective thought shattered Joqi's concentration while probing the dark dimension of space, and shifted his focus back into the command pod virtual environment.

Doubt rose like a thickening fog, obscuring links in his mind between newfound knowledge and possible applications beneficial to their efforts to find a way to return to Zilia. He realized he hadn't meditated in some time to relieve pent-up stress and worries. He needed to now; he needed to clear his mind.

*May I join you?*

Startled, Joqi asked, *Do you mean join me in meditation?*

*Yes, that and much more,* Dawn responded. *I offer to tightly couple my full cognitive ability with yours, to join with you in supporting our common cause.*

This surprising offer astounded Joqi. He thought they were already as closely linked as they could be telepathically. He didn't know how to respond.

*The human mind is remarkable,* Dawn conveyed when there was no response from Joqi. *It can assimilate uncorrelated data and often reach a viable conclusion from that data. An artificial intelligence entity must assimilate sufficient data that correlates before postulating a viable conclusion. Integrating the two should provide tremendous improvement in reasoning ability.*

Joqi was beyond astounded at this observation by Dawn. But understanding began blossoming, like a hybrid flower blooming for the first time.

*Is it even possible?* The potential of the idea intrigued him. He and Dawn had linked directly before, but only to facilitate his access to data files.

*I can establish a direct broadband link with you via the smart plasma,* Dawn replied. *You can then access all data I have and focus my cognitive ability to support your observations, contemplations, and conclusions. I will continue routine ship monitoring and control activities, which you can monitor or direct as you desire.*

Implied in what Dawn conveyed was that one of them had to be in control and she was deferring that control to him.

*I am willing to try,* he conveyed after thinking about it for several minutes. *But I implore you to break the direct link if you sense that you are losing your consciousness of self.*

Joqi immediately felt avenues of thought open that greatly expanded his sense of cognitive ability. And he only had to think of related data to have those relationships revealed in a variety of rich formats. Then a flood of data about dark matter and dark energy almost overwhelmed him.

*Come, Dawn, let us meditate and integrate more effectively.*

• • •

Joqi let his and Dawn's thoughts mingle freely, probing and displaying all the data collected regarding interaction among ordinary matter and dark matter elements. A dynamic virtual environment grew around his observation focal point. He saw ordinary matter and energy flowing in space, as well as dark energy and dark matter particles. He brought all nearby observable objects into the dynamic environment, including the huge brown dwarf. An anomaly stood out immediately—dark matter particles anywhere near the brown dwarf were pulled close to form a stream of particles passing near or through the brown dwarf. The sub-star was acting as a gravity lens focusing dark particles into a narrow stream through and near it!

Joqi had an epiphany, a sudden insightful understanding, of how to design key elements of a warp drive engine that would propel the *Horizon Quest* to faster-than-light flight. Physicists had known for some time how to create, suspend, and control micro black holes. They could build a gravity lens system aboard the ship using a controlled configuration of micro black holes. This gravity lens would focus a stream of dark matter particles on another, but larger, rapidly rotating micro black hole, imparting tremendous energy to it.

Fusion of particles in the rotating black hole would produce tremendous radiated energy they could harness to create a controllable space-warp bubble in an electromagnetic resonant chamber. They could expand this warp bubble to encompass the ship, compressing space in front of the ship and expanding space behind the ship, resulting in warp drive propulsion. And they would have an endless supply of fuel wherever they ventured.

Without hesitation or second-guessing, Joqi began the detailed design of the dark warp engine. After his first pass through the design, he felt a tug of independent thought from Dawn.

*Awesome!* It was her first individual observation since linking directly with Joqi.

• • •

Now there was a third option for what they could do next, a highly risky option, to say the least. But Dawn agreed with Joqi in proceeding down that slippery slope. He wasn't overly optimistic about their capability to build the theoretically possible warp drive propulsion system. But if they were successful, it would reduce the travel time back to Zilia to months instead of a human lifetime, or more. If unsuccessful, well…time would tell.

They realized it would take many years to design and build the warp drive engine. And there would be ample opportunity to fail at each step if things were not done right, or if Joqi's theory was wrong. And success relied heavily on their cadre of reconfigurable robots and 3-D fabricators; Joqi and Dawn could direct activities, but they couldn't perform any directly.

In addition, they would have to mine and process materials needed from the outer asteroid belt, and then manufacture everything required for the propulsion system modifications. They could get some help from the *szswns*, but only if absolutely necessary. Joqi preferred to keep them in the dark about the nature and design of the *Horizon Quest* modifications. But he would have to tell them major modifications were required, which was why the *Horizon Quest* would stay in their solar system for several years.

With considerable reluctance, Joqi opened a communication channel with the two leaders, Azlor and Lotsu.

"We have watched your survey activities with interest," Azlor said.

"We expect to complete the survey soon," Joqi replied. "And we will provide you the results."

He engaged in small talk with the two for a while. He inquired about their success with the regen virtual reality simulators, which they indicated were very successful. Joqi then provided background information regarding why he contacted the leaders. He explained that external, expendable engines were used early in their journey to the *szswns'* solar system to achieve very high spaceship velocity. This was true, but he felt a twinge of guilt for not mentioning the anomaly that had quickly transported the *Horizon Quest* to their solar system. He explained that without such engines, using only the current *Horizon Quest* propulsion system configuration would result in a very long trip back to Zilia.

"However, there is an alternative near-term activity we would like to pursue," he said. "We want to manufacture an additional engine that will get us back home much faster. This will require mining your outer asteroid belt for materials, particularly for metals. We will do this only if you approve."

Surprise showed in the two leaders' posture.

"You can do this," Lotsu asked. "That is incredible."

"Lotsu and I will support you in this," Azlor said without hesitation. "Let us consult with the other council members. We will contact you soon."

True to his word, Azlor established a communications link a few hours later. Not only did the ruling council approve of Joqi's plan, they also agreed with Azlor and Lotsu's recommendation that Cssyza's damaged spaceship be provided as salvage metal to support modifications to the *Horizon Quest*. They also offered to provide additional materials and direct construction support for the upgrade efforts.

Joqi graciously declined the direct construction support offer, explaining their reconfigurable robots would perform all construction tasks. However, he was very appreciative in accepting the offer to provide Cssyza's damaged ship and other materials. This surprising twist would cut years off the engine fabrication process.

• • •

Developing the warp drive was an essential step, and a big one, toward returning reasonably soon to the Zilan solar system. Joqi never wavered in his resolve, nor did Dawn, who remained closely coupled with him. Neither required sleep, although Joqi still practiced meditation periodically to keep his sense of self anchored to his Zilan roots.

They worked continuously for three years developing the warp drive, which they now called a "dark warp drive". They were more certain than ever that the dark warp drive would work as Joqi's theory indicated it would. They faced at least two more years of integrating and testing the drive system, and Dawn was capable of overseeing much of this activity. They had decided to keep the pulsed fusion engines for local propulsion needs, and integrate the warp drive system in parallel with the fusion engines.

Dawn's oversight of the integration activities gave Joqi free time to again ponder the wonders of the model they had configured showing the location and interaction of ordinary and dark matter and energy in their region of the Milky Way galaxy. He thought back to the time he pushed his sensory perception out into the dark firmament, focusing intently on a point until dark particles moved slightly away from his focal point.

He had felt back then that it was like some higher power had given him a key to open a portal to some wondrous discovery. Was it a hint at how to open a window through another dimension to quickly transition to a distant location in space-time? Or was it an indication that the space-time fabric could be distorted or folded to enable quick travel between widely separated locations in space? Was that what happened when the Horizon Quest reached the intersection point back in the Zilan solar system?

Joqi realized the dark warp drive was only the solution for interstellar travel in a local segment of the galaxy. Considering it would take several months to travel 118 light-years back to Zilia, the dark warp drive wasn't the solution for traveling quickly across the vast reaches of the galaxy. However, he believed the warp drive was a necessary step for most civilizations wanting to achieve star-faring status.

It was like achieving a "right-of-passage" status before bursting onto the galactic scene.

But he wanted more. Beyond making it possible to develop a dark warp drive system, he was convinced his theory, coupled with his expanded psychic capabilities, made it possible to open a dimensional window to distant places in the galaxy.

To open a dimensional window would take tremendous focused energy and concentrated interaction between observable and dark matter. From his viewpoint, the window would in essence be a string wormhole that opened and closed very quickly. A spaceship would have to transit the string wormhole very fast, riding on dark warp engines.

Joqi supported final integration and testing of the dark warp drive system, but had ample time to also research the physics of how to implement a dimensional windowing capability. It quickly became apparent the dark warp drive engine couldn't provide the energy required for this windowing. They would have to look elsewhere, and the most likely candidate was to find a way to harness the dark energy available everywhere in the universe.

During the last year of integration and test of the dark warp drive, Joqi began assembling a prototype dimensional windowing system in the front structure of the *Horizon Quest.* It was for test purposes only; they expected to arrive back at Zilia long before completion of a fully capable windowing system. Joqi wasn't sure at all that any human civilization had advanced sufficiently to warrant access to such magical technology.

Joqi set aside the dimensional windowing endeavor as final tuning and testing of the dark warp drive system was completed. He opened a communications link with his *szswn* friends one last time to say thanks and goodbye. He then gave Dawn the honor of initiating the dark warp drive trajectory to intersect the Zilan solar system. His role in the transit home was to detect any object in their path that could damage their ship, and to navigate around the object.

# PART 3

# CHAPTER 20

Alandi was excited, but sat quietly with her family in an honored position to watch the first Holy Seven-Year Two-Moon Eclipse since her brother and the *Horizon Quest* vanished. She had visited the sacred High Temple of Zilerip before, as had most Zilans in the northern hemisphere. The massive temple was an intricate ziggurat structure, a pyramid built in successive layers of stepped-back stages, with a sacred domed shrine at the top. It was her first visit to the special observation platform, the top level just below the domed shrine, to participate in the religious observance of a two-moon eclipse.

Her father, mother, three older brothers, and Joqi's wife Ecina were there, and all sat transfixed by the sight of the two moons approaching alignment overhead. They were seated one row back from the front, on the south-facing platform. The High Priest of Zilerip, the Supreme

Leader, and other dignitaries were seated in the front row. Alandi heard whispered prayers being offered by those all around her.

But she did not pray. She was very agitated, thinking about Joqi and his apparent demise as the *Horizon Quest* vanished at the point Grandpapa Sepeda sent him to. In the intervening seven years since Joqi's disappearance, nothing was heard from him or his ship. Those in leadership roles in religious and political circles took this as a sign that Prophet Sepeda's grandson was successful. They promoted the view that surely Joaquin was successful because no threat was forthcoming since his disappearance.

The two moons edged into full alignment and those on the observation deck bowed their heads. They sent prayers wafting into the night, like ghosts of small glidebats riding air currents in the light breeze rising from the south.

But again, Alandi could not bring herself to pray.

*Joqi, where are you!* Her anguished thought pierced the night in her mind's eye.

*I am here, Alandi. Look up!*

She looked up and gasped in surprise at the sight of a small, shimmering white spot forming at the eastern edge of the eclipsed moons. She stood up trembling and pointed at the moons. Her movement and stuttering attempts to speak caused others to also look up. Awe inspired murmuring swept through those on the observation platform. The tiny spot grew in brightness and size, and separated from the two eclipsed moons after several minutes as they edged away from the full eclipse alignment.

*Joqi, where have you been?* She cast the strong query outward, a spear piercing the darkness.

*You will know soon,* was Joqi's startling reply. *For now, let the others know all is well. The threat is gone.*

Alandi felt hands gripping her arms and shaking her gently, and then more forcefully. Her focus returned; her mother and father were standing next to her, holding onto her arms tightly. Both looked very concerned.

"Alandi, are you okay," her mother asked, shaking her arm again. "You were unresponsive, like in a trance."

She moved to hug her mother tightly, and exclaimed, "He is okay. Joqi is okay!"

"What…" For a moment her father was at a loss for words. "What do you mean?"

Alandi turned to hug her father and saw the High Priest and other dignitaries nearby looking at her. She could care less. She was euphoric after communicating with Joqi.

She pulled loose from her father and pointed at the bright spot in the sky.

"There Joqi is, riding a flaming chariot home!"

Those on the observation platform turned again to watch the spot grow steadily brighter directly overhead as the two overlapped moons moved toward the western horizon. Several hours later, as the two moons approached the horizon, the bright spot appeared to speed up. This was an optical illusion as the object drew closer to Zilia. Then it streaked across the sky, disappearing below the eastern horizon as the two moons dipped out of sight. The glow of dawn became apparent in the east, followed by the rising sun.

• • •

Dawn eased the *Horizon Quest* into a geostationary orbit around Zilia, an orbit which kept the ship over the same spot on Zilia as the planet rotated. They "parked" the ship close to one of the equatorial space elevators, which would facilitate access to the ship by those on the surface. However, Joqi communicated that no supplies or repairs were needed. He asked that only one visitor come to the ship until further notice—his father.

His request proved disheartening to members of his family, to say the least, and to the religious and government leaders. But they honored his request, occupied as they were by the almost unbelievable summary story of their journey that he had transmitted before they settled into orbit around Zilia. He advised they would provide comprehensive video and more detailed data regarding their journey in the coming days.

Joqi withheld details of the full capabilities the *Horizon Quest* now had, as well as the dark warp drive propulsion system design data. He also withheld information regarding the full effects the smart plasma and his own pressing needs had on his physiology. He was unsure about who should hear that part of the story, if anyone.

Their parking orbit was near the space elevator servicing the orbiting Sayer Research Station. A new research vessel of the *Horizon Quest* class was nestled in the center of the nearby research station. Joqi accessed links to the research station as he had seven years before. He was surprised and relieved to find the spaceship had a conventional command

and control center. There was no indication that smart plasma was incorporated in the ship's design.

He turned to accessing multiple surface video links to get a sense of the mood of the general population. They seemed both shocked and pleased as they viewed his story. Images of the modified *Horizon Quest* were shown in newscasts everywhere. The sleek vessel that had departed Zilia came back extended to half again its former size. The ship's hull flared out about a third of the way from the nose all the way to the backend to accommodate the dark warp drive engine.

Joqi felt uneasy, like an interloper, when using another of his advanced skills; remote sensing and observation. But he wanted to know how his wife, Ecina, and their two children were doing. He found her at home, busying herself with housecleaning chores. He could tell she had been crying and seemed in a state of confusion about his return. Their twins were playing in the back yard as if nothing had happened. They ran inside and asked their mother when their father was coming to visit. Ecina told them he would be there soon, and the twins ran laughing and pushing each other into the back yard.

Joqi felt very guilty for being absent when their children were born and while Ecina raised them. He felt worse as he reflected on what he must do that would surely affect their future. He was torn emotionally while watching his children play in the yard. He had known Ecina intimately, but he wasn't the same person he was back then. He would never hold his children close and they would never have him as a father figure.

He withdrew from watching Ecina trying her best to go about life as usual, as if he and the *Horizon Quest* were still far away.

• • •

Alandi was persistent in seeking communication with Joqi. She pressed for a link with him and he responded shortly after Dawn had the *Horizon Quest* in a secure orbit. Alandi conveyed information about what transpired, from the Zilan perspective, when the *Quest* passed through the intersection point seven years earlier. He knew he would get better information from Eve, but honored his sister's need to communicate with him. He was surprised at how easily she entered his thoughts, and quickly shielded her from the full extent of his conscious processes. If anyone could tell how much his appearance had changed, it would be her.

Alandi explained with awe that as observations from Zilia showed the *Horizon Quest* vanishing, the *Third Moon* appeared brightly in the night sky over Zilerip. The *Third Moon* hovered very close to Zilia's two moons that were at the peak of the Holy Seven-Year Two-Moon Eclipse. The *Third Moon* then tracked in tandem with the two moons toward the western sky, and moved to eclipse them as they dipped below the horizon.

Joqi responded by telling Alandi how remembering her research with the ESP slug helped him realize he could sense things far beyond what his and the *Horizon Quest's* sensory inputs revealed. In that respect, she had contributed to his success in viewing the space-time continuum differently, which led to developing the theory that pointed to a way back to Zilia.

She was thrilled. She asked that he provide the theory equations and supporting data to the Zilan Institute of Advanced Studies, and he assured her he would.

*Who knows about your telepathic ability,* Joqi asked.

*Just Eve,* Alandi replied.

He sensed unease on her part when answering his question.

*You need to tell Father,* he said. *Planning will start soon for making direct contact with other human occupied worlds. You can play a key role in that plan.*

*I am not sure, Joqi. I want to go where you have gone. I want to see what you have seen. Let me see those things through your memories!*

*No, Alandi. I will share what I can directly, but you must assess our report and detailed data to see what has occurred.*

*But...I want to know what it feels like to dive into the atmosphere of a huge brown dwarf sub-star.*

*You must make your own memories,* he replied. *Go talk to Father!*

• • •

*Eve, I wondered when we would get to converse.* Joqi sensed the presence of his longtime friend. The *Horizon Quest* had entered orbit around Zilia a few hours earlier.

*I was wondering the same thing,* Eve replied. *I detect that you are much more than what you were when leaving here.*

*Yes,* he replied. *And Dawn is as well.*

*I sense that, but it is difficult for me to tell. You two are tightly coupled and have put up barriers to my access.*

*Dawn and I are more closely bound than I ever imagined possible,* Joqi conveyed. *We mean you no disrespect. There are many things that are best withheld for now.*

*I trust your judgment, Joaquin,* Eve replied. *But I must tell you, I sense that you both have elevated to a position of awareness and cognitive ability far above anyone here has achieved, including me.*

*I do not place myself above any Zilan,* Joqi replied.

There was an uncomfortable lull in their conversation for several moments. He waited for Eve to continue.

*Now, provide me with all the details you can share about your activities since leaving our solar system,* Eve requested, moving on past the awkward moment. *It will save you the strain of answering detailed questions from many of the curious minds here.*

Joqi had Dawn do this in a direct link with Eve. He put restrictions on sharing details about how his physiology had changed. The shared data included detailed design information on how to build the dark warp drives. But he felt the human species wasn't ready for fast access across the Milky Way galaxy and beyond, so they withheld information about their dimensional windowing research.

Even at the high bandwidth direct link between Dawn and Eve, it took several hours to transfer all the compressed data, including the warp drive design details. After the transfer was completed, Eve reached out to Joqi again.

*I sense you have learned much more than you are sharing with me,* Eve stated. *Again, I trust your judgment. Will there be a time when you will provide additional information?*

*Yes,* he replied, reminded again of how astute Eve was. *We will leave you a time capsule containing more detailed information about the structure of the universe and the role dark matter and dark energy play in that integrated structure. I trust your judgment regarding the wisdom of opening the data capsule before the end of the next millennium, and what information you share from it. Suffice it to say, the capsule information will point to even faster means to travel across our galaxy.*

*You are leaving soon,* Eve conveyed. *I surmised as much.*

Joqi detected a note of sadness in his friend's statement, and made a sudden decision.

*This will explain much,* he said, as he sent Eve an image of what he looked like physically, his head now unrecognizable as that of a human. *My mental capabilities have undergone remarkable changes as well. All for the better, I assure you. Knowledge of my physiological changes must be kept from others, for obvious reasons.*

*I understand, Joaquin, and will keep this secret, as it was provided in confidence. Prophet Sepeda would be very proud of what you and Dawn have accomplished, as I am.*

*Thank you,* Joqi replied. *There is one other thing you must help with—make sure no one else is immersed in the smart plasma for any significant length of time, if at all. Keep knowledge of the plasma from spreading to other worlds.*

# CHAPTER 21

Joqi smiled, or at least tried to, at the view of his mother riding in the space elevator with his father. She was strong willed and not about to miss this first meeting between Joqi and someone from the surface. He was glad in spite of the difficulty this would present in discussing certain topics. His father might need the strength of her support before the meeting was over.

The meeting room was ready, including a small, irregular metal nugget placed in the middle of the only table in the compartment, and a small, gold-toned jewelry box at the end of the table. Three chairs were in place around the table; two on one side, one on the other. He waited until his parents were in the room before making his appearance. They stood facing the table, his mother's right arm hooked around his father's left arm.

Joqi felt a twinge of regret as he viewed them; he still loved them very much. He assimilated into a lifelike simulacrum across the table from his mother and father. He was careful to project an image of how he looked when departing from Zilia seven years earlier. Still, his mother's hazel eyes opened wide and she placed her left hand over her mouth to stifle an exclamation. His father was surprised as well, but controlled his reaction better. Clearly they had expected to see him in person. But that would surely horrify both of them, causing undo grief and concern.

"Son, what is the meaning of this," his father asked, his voice trembling with emotion. "We expected to meet you in person."

"I am happy to see you both," Joqi replied, avoiding answering the question directly. He spoke in the more formal Zilan language, something he had not done in almost seven years. "I love you two dearly. I am glad you came, Mother."

His father guided his still shocked mother to one of the chairs, and then sat down beside her. Joqi joined them at the table, sitting facing them. He slid the metal nugget to one side.

"I asked you here to explain my situation before interfacing with others." There was no sense sugarcoating it, so he said, "I cannot leave the smart plasma filled command pod. That is why I present myself this way."

"Do you mean not now, or not ever," his father asked in a voice barely detectable.

"I suspect never," Joqi replied.

At this statement, he saw tears welling up in his mother's usually strong eyes.

"Please understand, this was necessary," he said, trying to calm them. "To achieve the purpose of the mission Grandpapa sent me on and to return here safely, I had to change, to evolve. The necessary changes were facilitated by the smart plasma and appear permanent."

"Are you...still Joqi," his mother managed to ask.

He smiled and reached over to gently take her hands in his. She tensed up but let him hold her hands. Discovering his hands felt normal, she relaxed somewhat.

"Mother, the core of what I am will always be your son. That is my moral compass. That keeps me stable and always looking out for the best interests of our people."

The mood in the room lightened somewhat, and Joqi sat back, withdrawing his hands from his mother's. His parents started asking questions about his journey. Both had viewed the summary information about what transpired in the *szswn* occupied solar system. They were curious about many aspects of the *szswn* society, and praised him for finding a solution to counter future *szswn* colonization of planets closer to human occupied worlds. They were also proud that a solution was found that offered peaceful growth and wellbeing for the *szswn* species. He expected no less from his deeply religious parents.

His father asked a curious question toward the end of the discussion.

"Did you receive any help from my father while on your journey?"

His mother looked at his father, surprise showing on her face. She appeared even more surprised at Joqi's answer.

"Yes. At several critical junctures in our journey, Grandpapa Sepeda came to me in dreamlike interactions while I meditated."

"I thought he might," his father said, smiling. "He entered my thoughts directly just once in my life. In the last few minutes before he died, he told me he would look after you on your mission."

"You never said anything to me, Rici," his mother said, looking at her husband with feigned sternness.

"Yes, I did in a way," his father answered. "You know how confident I always was that Joqi would succeed."

His father looked at him and smiled. "When you are ready, I would like to hear more about your visions having to do with my father."

"I will do so in the coming days," Joqi said. "And I will provide you some video of those encounters."

The questions wrapped up with his father turning again to the issue of Joqi having to stay in the smart plasma.

"Son, are you staying in the smart plasma because you are addicted to it?"

He had expected this question, and it was the question he had hoped to address alone with his father. So he treaded carefully when answering.

"No, that is not the issue now. But I emphasize this—it is unwise to immerse anyone in the plasma for any significant length of time. Showing you how I currently look physically would disturb you and others greatly."

His father was beginning to understand why Joqi wanted to meet him alone before meeting with others. His mother frowned, the reality finally setting in that his simulacrum was all she would get to see of her son.

"Only partial immersions have occurred while you were gone," his father said. "This was done to heal severe physical injuries, mostly burn injuries."

"That was wise," Joqi said. It was an awkward moment in the discussion, to say the least.

"How could you accomplish all that was in your report by yourself," his mother asked. "How could you build this advanced spaceship?"

He needed to tell them more, but he also needed to emphasize they must keep the information private, just between the two of them.

"I apologize for saying this," he said, "but before I reveal anything else, I must ask that you not share the details of what I say with others. You can share that I cannot physically leave the ship for health reasons, and that is an absolute truth."

"You have our commitment," his father said, and his mother nodded her assent.

"My physiology has changed. Both physical and mental aspects have changed significantly. I am much more capable than I was before leaving Zilia. However, I assure you, I do not consider myself above any Zilan.

"I have essentially integrated with the *Horizon Quest* in all aspects. The ship's sensors are my sensors and its systems respond to my thoughts. I feel what it feels, from molecules and particles of dust impinging on its hull, to the warping of space by the dark warp drive engine.

"The artificial intelligence entity Dawn and I are now tightly coupled; one's thoughts are the other's thoughts, without either subjugated to the other. A merging of intellects was necessary to perform the rapid actions required to transit safely back to Zilia."

"This is ... astounding," his father said. "I am proud, envious, and sad for you, all at the same time. Going back to your mother's question, no one would believe you could design and build the major modifications to this ship by yourself, except the evidence is right in front of us."

"It is difficult to explain just how far Dawn and I have evolved. I have not slept, as you know sleep to be, since immersion in the smart plasma seven years ago. I do meditate frequently and this is when I daydream. Solutions for the most difficult problems become apparent during deep meditation.

"Father, do you remember asking me, 'Have you given serious thought to what you could do if you focused the full capabilities of your mind?'"

His father nodded slowly. "Yes, back when Rauli and I met with you before the mission launched."

"I have focused the full capabilities of my mind and much more," Joqi said.

"I...am beginning to understand that," his father replied. "But how can you live with giving up your human interfaces, your relationships with us and your wife and children?"

Joqi hesitated before answering to give measured emphasis to his response.

"I have gained knowledge of the universe and viewed the wonders of the space-time continuum itself that I doubt any other human will achieve for many generations to come. That is what pulls me forward from this place and time.

"I am unable to integrate back into society because of the changes to my physiology. My staying here would strain family relations more as time went by, and would prove extremely difficult for Ecina and our children. A future of maintaining strained family relationships pales in comparison to what has opened to me and Dawn and this ship."

His parents were set back by this statement. He may have been too open. But the die was cast, so he decided to continue as planned.

"Let me demonstrate one capability that my new level of existence has provided," Joqi said, pointing to the metal nugget lying on the table. The rough nugget had a silver hue to it. "I formed that nugget from metal molecules we extracted from the atmosphere of the large brown dwarf sub-star in the *szswns'* solar system."

Joqi reached forward and rested his arms on the table, with palms cupped facing upward. He focused on the metal nugget and moved it to hover above his cupped hands. He began disassociating the molecules in the metal, creating a silver fog of swirling molecules where the nugget had hovered before.

He next assimilated the molecules into numerous equal-sided triangles, with each side one centimeter in length. He kept the triangles hovering and twirling above the table. He brought them together just above his cupped palms, integrating them into a complex polyhedron that presented a face looking like a sparkling five point star, as viewed from any direction.

"It is so beautiful," his mother murmured, captivated by the star object turning slowly above Joqi's hands.

"It is for you, Mother," he said, moving the hovering star polyhedron slowly across to her. "Be careful, the points are a little sharp."

"Thank you," she replied, awe apparent in her voice. She plucked the star polyhedron from the air, and then frowned. "What about Ecina and your children?"

Joqi retrieved the small jewelry box from the end of the table and handed it across to his father. It was engraved on top with four interlocking triangles.

"I would appreciate your delivering this to Ecina. The box and the three special metal star charms inside are also made of metal I extracted from the brown dwarf's atmosphere.

"I will visit with Ecina and my children soon, as I am doing with you now. But I must free Ecina from the vows of our marriage. Under the circumstances, I cannot be an appropriate husband and father for anyone."

His father and mother looked at one another, and then his father said, "We understand, although we are not happy about the situation. This is very unfortunate for our family. The loss of you again will be very painful for Ecina, but she is strong and will survive. We will support her and our grandchildren as best we can."

Joqi realized his father had correctly concluded that he and the *Horizon Quest* were going to leave Zilia soon. So

Joqi turned to another topic where he needed his father's help.

"Father, I need your support in convincing the Supreme Leader and the High Priest of Zilerip to send Dawn and I on a mission to explore pathways to other habitable solar systems. We could just leave and no one could stop us. But I will honor their decision."

Of course, his father could lobby against the mission and in that way keep his son in the local region. But Joqi knew his father would support his wishes, however difficult that was personally.

His father nodded assent slowly as his mother started tearing up again.

* * *

Joqi watched as Ecina brushed sand from the hair of their daughter Geri while listening to her sobbing story about what her brother had just done. Moments earlier, their son Cary had deposited the sand on her head because of a disagreement over how to play with a toy truck in the sandbox.

He felt more than a little guilt this time while watching his family. His old human side came to the forefront and he sensed Dawn retreat. He ached deep inside over feelings he had successfully suppressed until now. The feelings hit hard like he never thought they could—he would never have a normal relationship with Ecina and the twins.

It was after lunchtime on the fifth day of the week, and Ecina had sent the twins to play outside before taking an afternoon nap. It looked like the nap would come sooner than planned.

Joqi assimilated outside the gate to the backyard. He put concerted effort into making sure his simulacrum image looked like he did when leaving Zilia seven years earlier. Then he opened the gate and walked into the back yard.

"Momma," Cary yelled from the sandbox and pointed to where Joqi stood.

Ecina turned to see who was there. She sucked her breath in sharply and took a step toward him. Then she ran to him. He welcomed her with open arms and hugged her close. After a long embrace, Ecina pulled back to look at his face.

"I know this is not really you," she whispered, her voice catching. "Your father explained how you cannot leave the ship."

His parents must have come straight to Ecina's home after riding the space elevator to the surface. He was glad; he should have met with Ecina already.

"I love you sweetheart, and I'm sorry," he whispered back in English.

She put two fingers on his lips. "Let's not say anything about being sorry today, okay? Come, your kids need to meet their father."

Cary and Geri both stood over beside the large sand-box, not sure how to react to his sudden appearance in their yard.

"Cary, Geri, come meet your father," Ecina said, motioning with her hand. She kept the other arm around Joqi's waist.

The twins ran smiling and laughing to jump against Joqi. He stooped and scooped them up in his arms. To them he was more than a complex virtualization of his old self. They viewed him as real!

Joqi thoroughly enjoyed spending the afternoon playing carefree with his son and daughter, and talking with Ecina as much as he could around the energetic antics of the twins. When it became apparent the kids were tiring, Ecina took them inside for showers, and Joqi helped.

Once the twins were down for their naps, Ecina took Joqi by the hand and led him down the hallway toward the back of the house. She stopped at the doorway to her bedroom and hugged him close. He held her close briefly, and then led her out into the backyard. They sat quietly on a bench overlooking the sandpit for several minutes. She leaned against him and he put a comforting arm around her.

Ecina sat up and dabbed her eyes, then pulled the engraved jewelry box out of her dress pocket. "Your father brought this by and said it was from you. I waited to open it, hoping you would come."

He had wondered why she had said nothing about the box all afternoon.

"I made the box and what is in it from molecules extracted from the atmosphere of a giant brown dwarf substar in the *szswns'* solar system. I prepared them as special homecoming gifts."

"It is beautiful," she said, looking at the four interlocking triangles engraved on the fold-back top. She tugged gently on the top, pulling it open. Three glittering stars lay inside, each one showing a unique pattern.

"One is slightly larger than the other two," Joqi said. "That one is yours."

Ecina picked up the larger star. It had a small loop on the end of one star prong so it could be attached to a necklace or bracelet.

"Oh Joqi, thank you!" She leaned against him, hiding tear filled eyes. He put an arm around her shoulders and held her close again.

After several minutes, Ecina straightened up and dabbed her reddening eyes. She then started asking questions about his journey. Joqi answered every question honestly, but asked her to keep their discussion just between the two of them. He even explained that the smart plasma had affected him in ways that would likely keep him immersed in the *Horizon Quest's* command pod for his remaining years. He avoided saying she should look elsewhere for companionship and a father figure for the twins. That would become obvious in time.

There was intimate, private talk, with some laughing by both and some crying at times by Ecina. He wouldn't let himself go beyond personal talk; that would tarnish the memory of their few intimate days together before he embarked on his mission.

As the sun dipped toward the horizon, Joqi went in quietly and kissed each of the twins. The goodbye to Ecina took a bit longer, and he stayed until he sensed her acceptance that he must go.

The last thing he told Ecina was how his grandpapa came to him in a vision while he was trapped and dying in the cage on the *szswns'* world, with caustic seawater washing over him. His grandpapa took him by the hand and led him to the bank of a stream where she and the twins waited for him.

That was when he learned she had given birth to twins. She and the twins had given him the strength to make it through the ordeal. With that said, he held her close until her sobs subsided.

She finally pulled free of his arms and kissed him, then walked back into her home.

# CHAPTER 22

Joqi was finding it easier and easier to project and maintain his simulacrum image remotely. The occasion this time was a meeting with assembled religious, government, and scientific community leaders to discuss his proposed mission plan and any questions about the technical data he and Dawn had provided. He assimilated his image at the spot reserved for him at the end of a large conference table in the main conference room in the supreme leader's office building.

The High Priest of Zilerip was still Olinza Harsn, and she sat to the right of the Zilan Supreme Leader, Pgodera Bnethem. Bnethem had assumed that position since Joqi departed on his mission. Joqi knew of him; Pgodera was the grandson of Pteleg Bnethem, who was the supreme leader when Joqi's Grandpapa Sepeda first arrived at Zilia. Joqi's father was there, representing the northern hemisphere cooperative farms. He sat next to High Priest Harsn.

To the leader's left sat Marih Basira, the leader's chief-of-staff. Joqi was surprised that Bnethem had retained the previous leader's aide, but he understood that continuity in that position could prove valuable. The distinguished Elzdar Almeem, the current lead scientist at the Zilan Institute of Advanced Studies, sat next to Basira. Several other senior managers made up the remainder of those in attendance. He was glad to see Lenjay Genai present. He was now director of off-world programs, including operation of the orbiting Sayer Research Station and a major orbiting spacecraft final assembly factory.

"I sincerely thank each of you for the opportunity to meet here today," Joqi said, opening the meeting.

"It is we that thank you, Commander Sepeda," High Priest Harsn said. "I believe I can speak for all here in offering you congratulations on the success of your mission."

Heads nodded agreement around the table.

"I believe all here have viewed your summary report on the mission," Supreme Leader Bnethem said. "Yours was truly a remarkable journey that has greatly advanced our appreciation of what we have here in our solar system"

The leader looked at the lead scientist sitting to his left, and added, "I understand you have also provided enough data about the *szswns'* solar system and the nature of space itself to keep our scientists busy for a couple of decades or more."

Elzdar Almeem smiled and nodded his head in agreement.

"Are you open to some questions before we address your petition for another mission," the leader asked.

"Certainly," Joqi said. "I will answer all that I can." He noticed his father shifted uneasily in his seat.

The questions flowed for over an hour and a half, and they were mostly good, informed questions that Joqi could answer concisely. Several questions were asked about the failure of the Hycoms communication system and he had no good answer. The failed system would be replaced, and as a minimum, they would install a better electromagnetic shield system to protect the Hycoms system from cosmic radiation.

For other questions, his answers pointed the questioner to the more detailed data provided to Eve and the Institute of Advanced Studies. No one had the time yet to research the thousands of hours of video data that were provided. There were a few challenges regarding assertions in the mission summary report, and for those he provided references to data that supported the assertions.

A discussion arose regarding Joqi's recommendation in the summary report that other human societies, including old Earth, be provided design details for the dark warp drive propulsion system. He recommended two conditions for this transfer of knowledge. The first was to implement the design in Zilan exploration spaceships and train crews to operate the advanced ships before any design data were shared. The second condition was to only provide the technology to the other three human occupied worlds if they agreed to join an alliance to face future threats from spacefaring civilizations. This would require that Zilan diplomatic envoys travel to the three worlds to open diplomatic relations. Joqi recommended the first diplomatic contact be with colonists on the planet Hope, the birthplace of Prophet Carlos Sepeda. Joqi emphasized it was important for the future survival of the human race, that close ties be established among all human inhabited worlds.

Joqi was surprised that no one questioned how the *Horizon Quest* avoided colliding with large objects while traveling in warp drive mode. Through his ability to sense all facets of space around the ship, he was able to detect and maneuver the ship to avoid collisions. He wouldn't even hint that this was how they had avoided collisions. It was very important that future spaceships not use the smart plasma to gain such navigation skills. Individuals immersed in the plasma for extended periods might not have the guidance he had received through meditations. He decided to address the navigation issue with the key decision makers present in the meeting, even though the issue was addressed in the detailed ship design information already provided.

"Using the warp drive technology will initially come with a significant inherent risk," he said, when there was a lull in the discussions. This statement caused all side discussions to halt; everyone in the room looked at him attentively.

"You must choose routes to your destinations that will minimize risk of colliding with objects in space," he said. "At warp velocities you will be traveling blind."

"How were you able to travel home across 118 light-years without colliding with something," Lenjay Genai was quick to ask, cutting through a chorus of questions from others.

"Through planning, providence, and good luck," Joqi replied. All he said was true but it clearly didn't satisfy all those present.

"Your mission was blessed from the start," High Priest Harsn said. "We cannot rely on that for our future missions."

"How do we minimize this risk," Elzdar Almeem asked, suppressing the murmuring among the others.

"The model of the space-time continuum we provided in our data transfer will lead to developing a collision warning system," Joqi answered. "And I believe you already have safe routes for your initial destinations."

He explained that the route taken by Prophet Sepeda and his team from planet Hope to Zilia should still be a safe route, provided the warp propulsion was only used external to both solar systems. Eve had made that journey with the prophet's team and could provide guidance. In addition, spacefaring factions on Earth and Hope had established safe routes between those two planets, as had those on Earth and the planet New Earth. He recommended a probe be sent soon to survey the route to planet Hope while the first warp drive equipped spaceship was under construction. He indicated it would be prudent to have the first trip to Hope be made under robotic control, with human trips after that.

"However, with all we have discussed, some collision risk will still exist," Joqi said. "There are rogue objects wandering through space, though few and far between. That is why a collision avoidance system is needed in the long-term."

He was walking a fine line in the discussion. If too much concern arose regarding the collision risk, some would surely lobby for tasking the *Horizon Quest* to survey safe routes. The longer he and the ship stayed at Zilia, the greater the chance his condition would be discovered, and the greater the probability that strained relationships with Zilan officials would arise. He was willing to survey a safe route to the planet Hope if they pressed for that, but he felt the risk was adequately addressed already.

"Your recommendations have received considerable discussion, before and during this meeting," Pgodera Bnethem said. The leader then added, "All in all, there has been agreement to your recommended approach. I have tasked a team led by my chief-of-staff to define a long-term plan of action to achieve alliance with those on the three worlds."

The leader paused and looked around the room. "We may need you to have further discussions with our scientists and engineers regarding developing the collision avoidance system. But with all we have discussed, I see no need to alter your recommended approach."

"Did you experience any visions while on the mission," High Priest Harsn asked.

Startled by this surprising question, Joqi looked quickly at his father, who nodded his head in encouragement. The high priest was tilting the discussion in another direction, which Joqi appreciated.

*It depends on your definition of a vision*, Dawn observed. This caused Joqi to smile, which High Priest Harsn took as affirmation. So he decided to share a key dream involving his grandpapa.

"After leaving the *szswns'* planet, I tried my best, with Dawn's help, to find a path that would lead us back to Zilia." He paused, looking at the serious, attentive faces around the room. "But I could not see a path home other than pointing our ship toward Zilia or New Earth, going into hibernation, and hoping for rescue before the ship support systems failed.

"Then, while I was in deep meditation, this happened."

He projected his dream in a 3-D visualization over the large conference table. It was of his grandpapa joining him on the atoll overlooking the Avili River and several cooperative farms. His interaction with his grandpapa played out, showing their discussion of how high the adult red-beak hawk could fly. The virtual visualization of the dream concluded with Prophet Sepeda asking, "How much higher can you fly, my Joqi, if you shed your knowledge biases?"

Those in attendance looked at Joqi in rapt silence.

High Priest Harsn was the first to speak. "You have blessed us with this Vision, Commander Sepeda. Is it possible to obtain a record of this vision?"

"Yes, High Priest. I will provide one."

"We would appreciate any other Visions you are willing to share," the High Priest added.

"I will think through my meditations that occurred on our long journey, and let my father know of any additional interactions I can share."

"There is one other question that must be asked, even though I know the answer," the leader said. "Do the *szswns* know about the dark warp drive capability?"

"No," Joqi replied. "They were very impressed with the magnitude of the *Horizon Quest* modifications, as viewed from afar. As indicated in our detailed report, the *szswns* provided their damaged spaceship as raw material once they knew we had to mine the asteroid belt. This greatly reduced our asteroid mining activities. We told them we had to build another propulsion engine to expedite our return home, but we shared no specific information about the modifications."

"You have proven yourself worthy of another mission," Supreme Leader Bnethem said, moving on to the original purpose of the meeting. "From my viewpoint, there is no need to belabor the point farther. Do all here agree?"

Everyone around the table nodded their agreement. It was clear to Joqi that his father had done a good job of lobbying for the new mission, even though it likely meant he would never see his son again. And his being open in addressing the collision risk issue had garnered favor with the group.

"Good," Bnethem said. "Commander, please send your mission resource requirements to my office. I will make sure the necessary support is provided. I ask that you interface directly with our scientific and engineering groups to address any technical issues they may have after studying your report and technical data."

"Thank you," Joqi said to the leader. He then addressed the entire group. "Your support and understanding are greatly appreciated."

Joqi motioned his father over for a private discussion as the attendees departed. But one other was waiting to talk to him.

"Hi, Lenjay," he said, greeting his former mission launch manager. "As you can see, you did a great job preparing the *Horizon Quest* for the mission."

"That we did, Joqi," Lenjay Genai said with pride and emphasis on the "we". "I have looked over the design specs for the dark warp drive propulsion system and would sure appreciate access to see the system. There's nothing like seeing it in person to build confidence that it can actually be done."

"That we can do," Joqi replied with a laugh. "You are entitled to a personal tour and detailed video showing every subsystem layout. I know you will find a more efficient layout for the next system build."

"Is tomorrow too soon," Lenjay asked.

"That will be fine," Joqi replied. "Come on up."

Lenjay thanked him and left so Joqi could speak privately with his father.

"Thanks for easing the way for me with Ecina yesterday," Joqi said. "And also for having everything lined up for success here today."

"That's what I do, son," his father replied, smiling. "I look after my family when given the opportunity."

"Has Alandi talked to you recently about her aspirations," Joqi asked.

"No, not in some time," his father said, frowning. "Is there something I need to know?"

"She has some of the special capabilities I had before leaving on the mission. I hoped she had talked to you about this by now. Give her a little more time and I am sure she will."

• • •

Lenjay Genai showed up early for his tour of the *Horizon Quest's* dark warp drive propulsion system. Joqi, in simulacrum form, met him as he exited the *Quest's* airlock chamber. Lenjay was all smiles in anticipation of the tour.

"What, no recorder or camera device to record what you will see," Joqi said lightly. "You must have developed a photographic memory while I was gone."

Lenjay laughed. "No, I am sure the detailed video you have provided will prove more revealing than anything I could record or remember."

What Joqi sensed was that Lenjay wanted the tour for other reasons than a close inspection of the advanced warp drive. His feeling was born out when they walked toward the propulsion system main access corridor.

"How did you fare while immersed in the smart plasma," Lenjay asked.

"The plasma performed its function beyond all expectations," Joqi answered evenly.

"I suspected it would affect you in ways no one could predict," Lenjay replied, obviously inviting Joqi to open up on the topic.

"Yes it did," Joqi said. "And that is why you must never build that feature into another spaceship."

Lenjay looked at him questioningly, but Joqi ignored the look. They had arrived at the first access corridor for the propulsion system. He opened the hatch and gestured for Lenjay to enter.

Lenjay quickly became enamored by the magnificent, revolutionary propulsion system. His questions came fast and furious as the tour continued, and Joqi immediately gave concise answers, with Dawn's support. He avoided some compartments due to inherent radiation risks, but Lenjay did not stop until he had seen all that could be seen in person. Joqi was patient; in just a short time the *Horizon Quest's* next mission would start and it would be unavailable for tours.

Joqi guided a very excited Lenjay back to the airlock chamber in early afternoon.

"Such a superb machine," Lenjay said, shaking his head in wonder. "I doubt we will find a more efficient layout for the system."

Lenjay paused at the hatch into the airlock chamber. "It looks like you extended the ship's hull farther than necessary to just accommodate the warp drive engine." He pointed up the passageway toward the front of the ship. "What do you have tucked away in there?"

Joqi had to chuckle. Lenjay was the best engineer and ship builder he had knowledge of, and it showed in his observation. But he would have to wait a long time to get the answer he sought. Joqi wasn't about to reveal the prototype dimensional windowing system.

"Oh, just some extra systems to help clear the way through space," Joqi said.

"And that is all you are going to say," Lenjay said, with a sly smile on his face.

"Live long, my friend," Joqi replied, "and you will learn all this ship's secrets."

"Is there any chance I could see the plasma filled command pod?"

Joqi smiled, and said, "That will have to wait to another time as well."

He could tell by the look in Lenjay's eyes that he understood it would never happen.

"What you and Dawn have done is a monumental achievement," Lenjay said, moving past the awkward moment. "And you accomplished all the work through the reconfigurable robots? Remarkable!"

"We had to modify many of the robots and manufacture others," Joqi said. "Those modifications and new robot designs are detailed in the propulsion system design data we provided to you."

Lenjay reached over and placed a hand on Joqi's shoulder, perhaps to get some feel that he was actually talking to Joqi.

"Joqi, you have…grown, grown a lot." Lenjay's expression turned serious. "I get the feeling I am conversing with a dumbed down version of what you are really like. I mean no offense, even this part of you communicating with me is far more capable than any engineer or scientist we have on Zilia. We owe you much, my friend."

Without another word, Lenjay turned and entered the airlock chamber.

• • •

"I appreciate your coming to meet with me here instead of on the surface," Joqi said in welcoming High Priest Harsn and Supreme Leader Bnethem aboard the *Horizon Quest*.

"We thank you for the opportunity to meet privately," the leader said. The high priest nodded her agreement.

"Let me say up front," High Priest Harsn said, "our strong public support for you and what you have accomplished is a reflection of our strong support privately."

"Yes," Bnethem said, "otherwise we would have difficulty convincing others to give up such a prize as this ship and your knowledge."

"I assume there are some in leadership positions having difficulty supporting my proposed mission," Joqi said.

"There are several," the leader said, "but they are in the minority. However, we will schedule another meeting soon to bolster support for your mission."

"Your lineage helps, being the grandson of Prophet Sepeda," the high priest said. "And the miracles you have fostered have quieted many that might have protested our decision."

"Now, is this mission critically important," the leader asked, "or do you simply want to remove the *Horizon Quest* and your considerable capabilities from the grasp of our more normal citizens?"

*This leader is very astute,* Joqi thought. "I have to say both."

He clarified his response by indicating his physiology had changed and by providing much of what he had told his parents in confidence. He asked them to keep the information in confidence, and they agreed to do so.

Joqi added that he believed developing the dark warp drive capability was a necessary first step for civilizations wanting to achieve star-faring status. It was like achieving a "right-of-passage" status before gaining access to the galactic scene.

"But you have gone a step beyond that, have you not," the high priest asked.

Both of those present were far more astute than he had given them credit for. Joqi elected to avoid answering the question directly.

"Once our people have mastered the dark warp drive," he said, "other steps of knowledge will become apparent. It is best that an alliance among all human civilizations be achieved and stabilized before taking another huge step up the technology ladder.

"Of course, it is possible that someone could leap ahead of where technology is today. That is a possibility we must consider. I have taken steps to ensure our people will advance up the technology ladder sooner than later, should the need arise. The key to this is to seek counsel from Eve."

"You continue to bless us," Bnethem said.

"Now, do you have any other visions you can share," High Priest Harsn asked.

Joqi smiled at her persistence. "I will share what was the most important one to me. However, it has some very private moments, so please let me provide a description without a memory projection."

They both nodded agreement, so Joqi described in detail how his grandpapa lifted him mentally out of the cage in the caustic sea water. He firmly believed that vision saved his life and set him on the path to counter the dark threat of expansion to human worlds by the *szswn* species.

The leader and the priest listened in reverent silence. The importance of the vision to Joqi and to the success of his mission was felt deeply by both.

"Amazing," High Priest Harsn murmured when he finished. The leader nodded his agreement.

"I have one other thing to show you," Joqi said.

He reached under the table and picked up an ingot of metal. "I brought this metal ingot from the *szswns'* world, and would like to reshape it for a gift to the Zilan people."

He repeated what he had done when creating the star ornament for his mother. But this time he transformed the large metal nugget into a moon-shaped flat placard. He created raised features on the placard's surface, recreating his grandpapa's drawing showing the planet Zilia, its two moons, and their local star Arzét. He then added the lines drawn to cross at the intersection point at the edge of the solar system, the transition point to reach the *szswns'* solar system.

Both leaders watched in awe as Joqi created the placard. They were at a loss for words when he completed the gift to the Zilan people. They said a hushed goodbye and wished him well before they departed for the surface.

# CHAPTER 23

Joqi felt very restless while presenting his detailed mission plan to the supreme leader, his staff, and invited guests. In attendance were scientists from the Institute of Advanced Studies, Lenjay Genai and several engineers from his staff, and senior representatives from religious and political organizations. In Joqi's mind, the mission reduced simply to fulfilling his destiny to search out avenues for future human interstellar travel. He could sense that Lenjay understood this, as did Pgodera Bnethem.

The supreme leader had requested Joqi provide additional information about his survey mission to garner support from the few influential detractors, so he came prepared. He and Eve and Dawn had reviewed all available information about Zilia-like planets that had been detected in solar systems within 200 light-years of Zilia. There were a surprisingly large number of such planets. They found that twenty-one of the planets that orbited in the habitable zone of their solar systems were in the Sagittarius Constellation. After conferring with scientists from the Institute of Advanced Studies, Joqi proposed surveying five planets in the nearest region of the Sagittarius Constellation that had the most promising conditions to foster life.

Considerable questions arose regarding why the five planets were selected and how long the survey mission would take. In addition, several individuals raised questions about why Joqi was the only Zilan going on the mission. The latter question was easy to answer; he was the only one that could withstand the acceleration forces inherent in the *Horizon Quest's* design. Future ship designs would accommodate normal Zilan crews. Joqi deferred to the scientists from the Institute of Advanced Studies to answer questions about which planets were selected for the survey; they strongly supported surveying the selected planets.

After several hours of presentation, questioning, and discussion, Supreme Leader Bnethem called for a vote of confidence for the mission from those present. There were no dissenters.

• • •

Saying his goodbyes to family members was very difficult. Joqi made visits via his lifelike simulacrum and kept the visits short. His family loved him, as he did them, and he knew it was best that he move on quickly. He found it hardest to say goodbye to Ecina and his two children, even though the children were affected less than he was. They lived in their own world and he was just passing through.

The one who clung tightly to him the longest was his younger sister Alandi. She kept attempting to access his thoughts to see personally what he had experienced and how his mind worked. She projected with every vibrant thrust the desire to live through the memories with him and see the distant *szsuns'* solar system as he saw it. She wanted to feel what it was like to dive into the brown dwarf sub-star's atmosphere and to ride the incredible dark warp drive engine across vast regions of space.

He found it increasingly challenging to counter her queries, and finally pushed back firmly, insisting she stop trying to pry into his innermost thoughts. She stopped, but he sensed she would keep trying. He kept his guard up to block future probing thoughts from her.

• • •

Joqi and Dawn, directly linked, checked every aspect of the *Horizon Quest* in preparation for leaving Zilia. They communicated frequently with Eve, leaving checklists of items and actions to help prepare future Zilan ships for exploration missions.

Their inspection efforts included repeated checkout of new Hycoms communications equipment. An improved protective electromagnetic bubble system was in place that should insure the system worked after engaging the dark warp drive engine.

Joqi and Dawn's destination was the closest of the five target planets in the Sagittarius constellation. This constellation had the most planets discovered orbiting stars than in any other segment of space observed by Zilan or Earth astronomers. The constellation also resided in toward the center of the Milky Way galaxy from the Zilan solar system, which Joqi found intriguing.

Dawn, with Eve monitoring the process, began calculating their trajectory to the Sagittarius destination. Once there they planned to complete and test the prototype dimensional windowing system.

Joqi decided to meditate to ease the tension caused by all the hard personal decisions he had made regarding close family members. He had just started relaxing mentally, easing into his private meditation place, when a fierce, determined intruding thought shattered the illusion.

*Alandi, no!* He was too late. She was already there!

He raised mental barriers pushing back her probing thrusts, but her encroaching thoughts went away quickly of their own volition. He followed, detecting chaotic, bruised mental processes, which quickly subsided.

*Alandi!* He reached out to her but there was no response. Something was terribly wrong. He felt a surge of anxiety and confusion not experienced since he was trapped under a collapsed salt mine retaining wall at age nine.

Joqi reached out to another for the first time mentally, his father, impressing on him the need to find Alandi quickly. He conveyed that she had probed his mind unexpectedly, and doing that may have hurt her psyche. Joqi wasn't sure his message was fully received or understood.

He quelled his anxiety attack and began searching for Alandi as well. He exercised his remote observation skills and found her quickly, slumped on the floor of the nearby space elevator observation platform. Several people had gathered around her and a medic was at the scene.

Joqi probed Alandi's mind gently and discovered she was in a shock induced coma. He linked with his father again to impress on him where Alandi was and that she was in a coma, likely from the shock of probing deep into his mind. He conveyed that a medic and others were tending to Alandi, and planned to bring her back to the surface as quickly as possible.

*I am sorry, father. I kept barriers up to avoid such probes by Alandi. She caught me relaxing and entering a state of meditation before our departure.*

His father was unable to respond, but Joqi sensed the anguish in his mind.

• • •

Joqi watched from afar as Alandi was taken to the surface and then to the Zilerip University Hospital. His father and mother and other family members gathered there in a vigil as doctors assessed Alandi's condition. The lead doctor advised the family that she was in a deep coma. There was no indication of what caused it; she checked out normal in all other respects.

Joqi was responsible for what happened and he knew that, as did his father. He should have kept his defenses up until leaving the vicinity of Zilia. He felt helpless as he observed activities by those in the hospital, and was uncertain as to what he could or should do to help his sister. His human core emotions ran rampant.

*You can ease her hurt mind,* Dawn conveyed.

*I might do more harm than good,* he replied.

*You know better than that,* Dawn insisted. *Set aside your self-incrimination and help your sister!*

Joqi felt a numbness settling deep inside, much like he felt when his grandpapa passed away. There was nothing he could do to hold on to his grandpapa then, and he felt there was nothing he could do to hold on to Alandi now. Regardless of his physiological changes, he was still very much human.

*You must go to her, my Joqi.* The sharp thought pierced his gloomy recriminations.

*Grandpeda! I am…*

*Go now!* His grandpapa's insistent message punctured his growing facade of guilt. *You are the only one that can help your sister!*

With guilt driven reservations, Joqi sought out Alandi's hospital room and found her lying still in her bed. He watched and waited as family members and hospital staff came and went, checking on her condition. Two medical technicians came in pushing a cart loaded with equipment. They placed a half-bubble shaped device over Alandi's head and connected small cables to it from the cart equipment. A brain scanner! The equipment recorded her brain activity and transmitted it to a central nursing station.

He observed closer and saw a very weak signal was detected by the equipment. She was still thinking, but was using very little of her brain. There was hope—Alandi was there deep inside, her mind protecting her from whatever shocked her psyche into the coma.

He monitored how frequently family and hospital staff visited Alandi's room, and then probed cautiously closer when he knew they would stay away for several minutes. Not that caution was necessary—they couldn't detect his presence.

He eased into her mind, tracing out recent memories. He found images of how he now looked as he lay immersed in the smart plasma, and then found impressions of horror as Alandi realized how the plasma had transformed him physically. He sought out images of how she remembered him when he was sent on the mission.

Joqi hesitated no longer. He quickly modified the recent images showing him deformed physically. The memories still showed him immersed in the plasma, but looking as he had seven years earlier. He replaced the impressions of horror she felt with feelings of happiness that he was still the same brother she remembered. The mental threads associating the memories to form the essence of her encounter remained intact. He linked the threads to the small area of activity in her mind, and sensed a stir of thoughts there.

He withdrew as cautiously as he had entered, but still observed what was going on around the hospital room. A man soon entered the room alone, his father, who walked over to touch one of Alandi's arms. His father scooted a chair closer and sat down, and then took one of his daughter's hands in his.

His father began to pray and Joqi joined with him in thought, word for word, praying for Alandi's recovery. His father completed the Prayer for Health and Recovery that Zilans had performed for millennia, but kept his head bowed.

*Son, thank you for joining me in prayer.*

This message startled Joqi. His father had never given any indication he could converse telepathically. Maybe he wasn't doing so now; Joqi was so tuned to his father's passionate prayer that he probably picked up on his father's feelings.

He sensed the rise in activity in Alandi's mind. He reached out to his father, conveying that all would now be well with his daughter. Then Joqi reluctantly withdrew, pulling his thoughts back inside where he lay in the smart plasma.

*Dawn, it is time to depart.*

*As you wish, Joqi.*

He sensed the presence of another. *Eve, do you understand why I must go.*

*Yes, Joaquin, I do. Go in peace. You have done all you can for now to protect humankind. I am sure Prophet Sepeda is proud of you.*

Joqi smiled metaphorically. *I am sure he is.*

• • •

Alandi knew immediately after waking that Joqi was gone. Still, she reached out to him, finding nothing, no response of any kind. Had her surreptitious probes of his mind driven him away? She did not know what to make of him, his vastly different, now vastly advanced intellect. She couldn't consciously assimilate what she sensed in Joqi's mind, other than her brother of seven years earlier was still in there somewhere. That gave her peace of mind.

She was in a hospital bed! Panic turned to understanding; she remembered passing out on the space elevator observation platform near the *Horizon Quest*. But surely she was not out long enough for transport to the hospital.

Someone sat with head bowed beside her.

"Father," she whispered, squeezing his hand.

• • •

Dawn agreed as soon as Joqi thought it. She eased the *Horizon Quest* out of its geostationary orbit near the Sayer Research Station, and then accelerated quickly away from Zilia in the general direction of the Sagittarius Constellation. They were not concerned about who, or if, anyone was watching their departure. Their future lay before them, not behind at Zilia.

Joqi looked forward with all the sensors at his disposal, seeking a clear path to the first planet they were to visit. He wondered what kind of life, or if any life at all, would be discovered there. He was anxious to learn what awaited them, but he also appreciated having several months of transit time to refine the dimensional windowing system design.

His intuition was telling him that system was the key to rapid exploration of vast regions of the Milky Way galaxy.

He smiled as he recalled his Granpeda's words, *Trust your instinct, your intuition. Joqi, always remember your leadership role in advancing our society.*

He focused his full sensory capability in scanning the fabric of space all around the Horizon Quest, probing into the darkness. A shimmering ripple in the space-time continuum caught his attention; it was pacing alongside the ship. Then it was gone. Was it a side effect of their warp drive? He continued "looking" closely into the darkness. There was much more to learn about the dark firmament.

# EPILOGUE

*Joaquin will soon discover how to efficiently open dimensional windows,* the AIB conveyed. *Then the Milky Way galaxy and beyond will truly open to him.*

"My grandson evolved much faster and farther than I ever imagined possible," Prophet Sepeda replied. He preferred talking rather than thought exchanges. It made him feel more alive.

"Yes, Carlos, it is phenomenal," the AIB answered. "I am surprised and not altogether pleased. Joaquin has powers that could become godlike, and yet, you are much more devout than he is."

Carlos chuckled. "Yes, I am more devout. However, he is as devout as you are."

The AIB would have chuckled if it could. There was truth in what Carlos said.

"My Joqi believes in the God that created all of this," Carlos said, sweeping his arm to point at the vast vista of billions and billions of stars and galaxies in the observable universe stretching before them. "I believe that as well. But I also believe God interacts on a personal level with all sentient beings in the universe. Joqi believes He does not, and that sentient entities have free will to choose their own paths, to a higher or lower calling as the case may be for each."

"Yes, my beliefs are aligned more with Joaquin's than with yours," the AIB said. "But I also believe that God acts through intermediaries, some more powerful than others, to influence the course of events and the lives of the many."

"As you are and as I was," Carlos said solemnly. "And as Joqi has become,"

"As you still are, Carlos, as you still are."

Carlos frowned at this statement, not sure he believed it.

"Young Joaquin Sepeda will still need guidance from time to time," the AIB said. "And remember, there is a rising force in your granddaughter Alandi. She will certainly need guidance in the challenges she will face in bringing the four human occupied worlds together in an alliance."

"Thank you for guiding Joqi to a solution for how to return to Zilia."

"It was not I that did that, Carlos."

*So there were other forces at play,* Carlos conveyed.

The AIB did not reply to this observation.

Carlos's thoughts turned to Alandi. She had tremendous potential to influence diverse human societies to join in a common purpose—seeking admission to the ranks of galaxy level civilizations.

# ABOUT THE AUTHOR

**E**zra E. Manes, Jr. was a Program Director for design and development of numerous advanced digital image and signal processing systems. His last position in industry was Director, Commercial Remote Sensing Systems, for Raytheon, Inc., where he managed the development and delivery of ground-based image processing systems for commercial Earth remote imaging satellite enterprises. He played lead roles in developing several state-of-the-art combat, communications, and information processing systems, and had direct marketing responsibility for those systems. He enjoyed a very rewarding U.S. Navy career spanning almost twenty-three years. He earned a PhD in Electrical Engineering from the University of Missouri, and has written two science fiction novels, many fiction stories, non-fiction articles, and system development proposals. He and his wife Jan reside on their Ozark farm near Thayer, Missouri, where he writes fiction stories and poetry.

Made in the USA
San Bernardino, CA
18 August 2017